I0548962

Triple Diamond

MOST WANTED

GEMMA SNOW

Most Wanted
ISBN # 978-1-913186-23-4
©Copyright Gemma Snow 2019
Cover Art by Erin Dameron-Hill ©Copyright January 2019
Interior text design by Claire Siemaszkiewicz
Totally Bound Publishing

MOST WANTED

Dedication

To the incredible friends I've made in the romance community. Your support and love are unparalleled and I am so lucky to have met each and every one of you.

Chapter One

"Quinn." Ev fisted his shirt. His seeking fingers slipped below the waistband of her panties and found the slick, wet heat there. It had been a long week for both of them, and the second they had made it somewhere more private than a conference room at the FBI headquarters for longer than a passing glance, they had ripped at each other's clothes and made it as far as the couch.

"So ready for me, baby," he murmured against her cheek, the brush of two--day-old stubble a potent, animalistic aphrodisiac that made Ev arch up and press into his fingers with desperate need.

"Damn it, yes," she ground out, wanting him to go faster, to do something, *anything* to alleviate the insane pressure building within her.

"Patience," he said, but the increased speed of his fingers deep in her body belied his control and Ev simply pulled him down for another blistering kiss, dragging his shirt free of his dress pants and fumbling to unbutton it while distracting her with those lingering, achingly slow strokes.

"I don't want to be patient," she said around his kiss, biting, licking, kissing, sucking wherever she was able to get her mouth. "I want you. Now."

Quinn chuckled, but the sound came out low and husky and she knew he was as close to the edge as she was, as desperate to take her as she was to be taken, and the knowledge of how much he wanted her sent a new, far more potent wave of arousal surging through her body. He slid his fingers free so he could stand to kick off his shoes and yank his pants and socks off in one fluid movement. Even in the soft light from an early dawn, his skin glowed, dark and golden, contrasting with light-blue briefs that did little to hide how much he wanted her. Those piercing green eyes, as much a gift from his one Irish ancestor as was his name, Quinn Langston, scanned hot and heavy across her whole body, perusing her one free breast and her spilled, mussed hair and swollen lips.

"I fucking love looking at you like this, Ev," he said, voice raw with honesty and rich with arousal. "I love seeing you all spread out and waiting for me." His words, or maybe the tone of his voice, sent a new tremor of lust down her spine, and she shifted to push her slacks from her thighs. Quinn beat her to it, coming down to his knees between her spread legs and pulling her pants free way too slowly. He tossed them to the side, then slid his hand up her leg, moving in torturous circles near, but not near enough, to her covered slit.

"For fuck's sake, Quinn." Forget formidable FBI agent—right now she sounded about as intimidating as a horny bunny rabbit. Quinn only grinned, a rare but totally killer smile bright across his devilish face.

"Just teaching you a lesson, baby," he managed, and before she could get a word in, he lowered his head to her pussy and lapped at her wet, silk-covered hole. Ev gripped the couch so hard her muscles screamed, but the pleasure washing over her, demanding she simply give in to the release, was too much, overwhelming and wild, and she knew she couldn't hold it at bay any longer.

"Come, Ev," he said, his mouth still so close to her pussy. "Come now, baby." And it was the tone of his voice that did it, bursting the dam of her pleasure until all she could do was ride the intense, ferocious wave, screaming his name as she did.

Quinn leaned on the back of the couch to bend down and kiss her, a smug grin on his face and rare laughter spilling from his mouth.

"Shh, banshee," he muttered around kisses. "You'll get Lucas all excited."

Right now, Ev wouldn't have been bothered if her director at the Bureau called her into work, let alone that her roommate was asleep down the hall. All she could think about was getting Quinn inside her. About five minutes ago.

"Now," she demanded, loving the humor in those green eyes, loving that she could be the one to make such a normally stalwart, serious man smile. "I mean it."

He repeated her words, mocking with gentle sarcasm, then he stripped himself of the white muscle tank he wore, exposing toned, powerful abs, dusted in a light strip of hair that led down to the waistband of his briefs. Quinn liked to tease her. He was not a man to cede control easily—not that she was all that good at it either—and he enjoyed pushing her to the breaking point. Ev wasn't going to deny that she liked being pushed. She sat back and simply indulged in the slow ease with which he slid his briefs down those dark, muscled thighs, exposing a thick, throbbing cock she couldn't seem to get enough of.

Then he was there, right there, sliding her panties down and away, then teasing her entrance and not slipping into her wet pussy like she so desperately needed him to do. He slid across her wetness and she rocked up to meet his touch, to somehow steal the connection he denied her.

"Say it," Quinn demanded, control wavering, need coloring his voice low and demanding. "Say it, Ev. Tell me what you need right now."

"Your cock inside me, goddammit." The words came out on a harsh breath. "I swear to *fuck...*"

In that moment, he pressed deep inside her, stretching her needy body, turning the word into an expletive of pleasure. He was big, long and thick and it took a moment for her body to accommodate his size, even after all the months of them catching each other on couches and beds, ships passing in the night. But she did adjust, then she rocked into him with abject desperation. Quinn clearly wanted to say something snarky, but his control was more than fraying now. It was cracking right through and Ev knew she had him exactly where she wanted him — buried balls-deep inside her.

Powerful, controlled, all-important Special Agent Quinn Langston was at her mercy, and damn if that wasn't some heady shit. Of course, in a thousand different ways she was at his mercy too, but the only one that mattered right now was the way he drove potent, impossible pleasure into her body with every stroke of his cock. Ev wrapped her legs around his waist, pulled him as close to her as she could and rode him as wildly and desperately as he rode her.

She was so close, so very near the edge of breaking, that when Quinn brought his hand to her breast, the movement rough and needy, and stroked her nipple, she fell out from under herself, giving in to the ride, thrusting against him once, twice and once more before she shattered around his cock. The pulsing tightness of her pussy brought Quinn right over the edge with her, and he let out a string of curses and released inside her, thick and hot and enough to chase aftershocks of pleasure through her body.

He leaned against the back of the couch, catching his breath while keeping his weight off her, then bent down to give her a kiss. His mouth tasted like her desire, another reminder of this insane, combustible thing between them that had been going on for so long before either of them had realized it.

"I'll get us a towel," he murmured into her hair. "Be right back." He was slow and careful when he pulled free from her body, and Ev missed the feeling of him instantly, her skin cold without his touch. It was odd, that. For so long, she'd been so accustomed to being alone, to having friends — close friends, too — but just a few months into this new thing with Quinn had her all sorts of topsy-turvy and thrown off her axis.

And it wasn't *just* that she cared for him. She did, deeply and recklessly, the kind of emotion that scared the ever-loving daylights out of her. But according to her sister Aurora, those kinds of feelings were the good scary and she could objectively see that. No, those emotions, the fear she might ruin her incredible friendship, the potential for heartbreak, for getting too close — those weren't what snuck up in the middle of the night and gave her doubts and insecurities about the future.

But she couldn't bring herself to think about the creepy shadow thoughts now, not in the early dawn, with streaks of pink and gold cutting through the blinds and giving the false impression it was warm outside. No, not in the much warmer afterglow of long-overdue lovemaking with her very hot boyfriend, thanks very much. There wasn't anything else to think about, not now and not ever.

Ah, but there is, isn't there? Because if there wasn't then why would you keep wondering if this is it?

But before she could flay herself for *that* ridiculous thought, Quinn came back into the living room. He kept his hair short these days. Back in their early weeks at Quantico, he'd gathered the near-blond afro into a ponytail at the base of his neck and even in those very first times they'd gotten to know each other, Ev had wondered how he would respond to having his hair pulled in the throes of passion like they had just shared. Of course, he looked too young with his hair like that, too much the volatile, angry veteran he'd once been. Now, five years later, Ev could sit back and appreciate how he'd aged like a fine wine, all beautiful cuts of shadow and lightness, high, strong cheekbones and full lips demanding to be sucked. Of course, he put out a scary-as-hell demeanor, but she knew what it took to bring a man like Quinn Langston to his knees.

Literally.

"You're looking like the cat that got the cream," he said with a grin just as smug. He joined her on the couch, wiping away the remnants of the morning's activities with a warm towel.

"More like the cat that got *to* cream," she said before she could stop herself. What would her coworkers say about her now? Quinn wasn't the only one who put on a hard-as-hell exterior when he went to work. Ev could not only be an unapproachable ice queen at the job, but she'd worked hard to perfect the look, just as Quinn and Lucas had both created personas for themselves from the early days, whether they knew it or not.

Quinn opened his mouth to respond, but her phone went off somewhere and Ev jumped up from the couch, only just realizing how cold the room was when the movement made cool air brush her nipples and goosebumps break out across her skin. She wrapped a blanket around her body and grabbed her pants, looking for the sound. Locating it in her pocket, she answered without looking at the name.

"Monteiro." *Do I really sound so out of breath?*

"Well, I certainly hope so, since I haven't heard any news of a wedding."

Relief made her shoulders sag and Ev settled into the couch, tucking herself under Quinn's arm. He tossed another blanket over her bare body and she snuggled closer to him.

"*Tudo bem, mãezinha?*" she greeted. "Why are you calling me this early? I thought Dad was working the night shift at the restaurant now."

"Night shift, *pah*." Her mother's energetic tone gave Ev the impression she'd been up for hours and had used as much control as was in her arsenal to wait until after the sun had risen to give her youngest daughter a call. "Evangeline, your father owns six of the most successful restaurants in the whole state and you call it a night shift." In truth, it was an old habit from when her father *had* worked the night shifts in other first-generation Portuguese restaurants when she was only a child, but Ev knew damn well why her mother insisted on pointing out the number and level of success of each of their businesses every time she called.

"I'm happy with my job, *mãezinha,*" she said. "And Quinn and I are still dating, before you ask."

Her mother *humphed.* "Well, as long as you're not married. But I do want you to know—Estela Patrício, her son is coming to town next weekend…"

"No, *mamã,*" Ev said, keeping her voice firm. It was the only effective method of communication. "I'm dating Quinn and I'm very happy about it. Now, is there something else? Because we have a plane to catch."

Her mama *tutted,* repeated the information about Estela Patrício's son, *a businessman,* gossiped about Ev's sisters, gushed about her brother then repeated the information about Estela Patrício's son one last time.

Ev glanced at the clock mounted above their useless fireplace.

"I've got to go now," she said, cutting through her mother's sentence. "We didn't land until three last night and I'm catching a flight in, like, an hour." More like four, but exaggeration was another tried and true technique where her *mamã* was concerned.

Finally, finally, her mother wished her safe travel, bade her visit—*not next weekend, mamã*—and hung up the phone.

Ev sighed and glanced up at Quinn. He grinned, the sated, amused grin she didn't see nearly enough of on his handsome face.

"Don't laugh at me," she muttered, but he reached out and tweaked one nipple at the same moment, which made her squeal and wiggle out of his embrace in a vain effort to protect herself.

"I'm not laughing," Quinn said, hovering over her on the couch like the sexiest predator she'd ever seen.

After a moment, though, he settled against her, fatigue outlining his handsome features. It was absurd they were even still awake right now. Still, her flight *had* landed just as she told her mother, nearly three in the morning. Quinn had been there waiting for her, after a week of them playing phone tag and sneaking in and out of the apartment while the other was dead asleep. They'd barely made it through the front door without ripping each other's clothes off and now it was morning — not that *morning* counted for a whole hell of a lot in their line of work — and all three of them had a plane to catch in just a few hours.

"Quinn…" This wasn't the first time they'd had this conversation and it wouldn't be the last.

"I know, I know, it's not 'cause I'm a black guy from the city." His humor was hollow and tired, but tinged with amusement.

"You're from Cleveland," she pointed out. "And it's not." Just as it wasn't the first time they'd trodden this well-worn territory. "It's only because you're not Portuguese. She wouldn't like me dating Lucas, either. Hell, she wouldn't even be okay with Patrick."

Lucas Vallejo would have given her mother kittens, but Ev's very white, very Western European boss Patrick Wickham wouldn't have passed the test, either. Ev was the only one of her *mamã*'s children to not bring home a Portuguese man, excepting her brother, who brought home different women with alarming regularity, and dear old *Mamã* was persistent in her task to single-handedly populate the Ironbound with the next generation.

She rolled her eyes. Her mother's antiquated ideals were still a solid presence in Ev's life, despite her being an Ivy League graduate with a top job in the FBI and approaching the birthday that would put her decidedly on the other side of her mid-thirties. "*Mamã*, she's old-school. Still hasn't forgiven me for moving to DC."

Quinn knew the spiel. In the months since they'd first moved their friendship into something more, they'd circled this conversation a dozen times, but it never made it any easier. Quinn's race, Lucas' race, Ev's sex — it had brought them closer together during those months at Quantico, surrounded by the pretty-boy country Captain Americas and the New England Ivy graduates who could have passed for their ancestors from two hundred years earlier. Being of any race other than white, or any gender other than male, put one at a disadvantage — a disadvantage that had led to one of the strongest bonds of friendship Ev had ever known.

"I know, baby," he said. He planted a kiss on her forehead and stood from the couch, moving toward the kitchenette with a slowness that betrayed his exhaustion. The city had been on high alert for terrorist activity after a series of phone calls, and Quinn, Special Agent for a Counterterrorism Fly Team under Lydia Brandenwell, who reported direct to the Secretary of Defense, had been busy in a way most civilians would never understand.

But she knew, simply by watching the slight limp in his left leg, an injury from an IED blast eight years earlier that tired more easily when he was fatigued, and the way his shoulders folded just a little. The only signs that Quinn Langston was running on empty.

"When did we buy this milk?" He pulled a suspect-looking half-carton from the fridge and held it up for her inspection. Ev grimaced and stood.

"I think the answer is too long ago. There's evaporated in the cabinet." Which was why she was still living in this apartment, had been even before she and Quinn had given in to their long-standing desires a few months ago. Between the three of them, Lucas, Quinn and Ev used the apartment about as often as one person did. Case in point, on closer inspection the milk was definitely chunky.

"We'll get something at the airport," Quinn said, tossing the whole thing into the trash without dumping it down the sink. *Good, way too early in the morning for chunky milk.*

"We should probably head out soon. TSA and all." *Ha.* She hadn't been on a commercial airline in years. Then again, she hadn't been on vacation in years. Still, when it was her boss and former trainer at Quantico, not to speak of one of her best friends, getting married, she flew her ass to Montana whether she was dead on her feet or not.

"Using you as a pillow," she said. "I don't remember when I actually slept last." *Which is probably for the better, since when I do sleep, I keep dreaming of...*

He nudged her out of the reverie and she leaned up to kiss his cheek, just as he went in for the kill, grabbing her around the waist and lifting her up with deadly aimed tickling fingers. Yeah, she was exhausted, sleep-deprived and headed for a flight into the middle of nowhere, trying to take down bad guys who kept coming back bigger and badder than before. But things were okay — they were better than okay. With Quinn Langston by her side, Ev had everything she needed to live a damn happy life.

Almost.

Chapter Two

Lucas brushed the loose, messy curls from his face and forced a smile. *Ha, that wouldn't even fly with Carly – or was she Kayla? – and she's only seen your face in the dark.* Which meant his two best friends in the world, the ones who had seen him through the worst of the worst in his life, would take one glance and force him into the therapy chair.

Coffee. He needed coffee. But he'd pulled himself free from possibly-called-Chloe's arms and stumbled into the bathroom to take a leak, only to catch sight of way more than he needed to see on his living room couch. For all intents and purposes, they should have left him at least one-third of the sofa that didn't have ass prints on it.

But he'd caught them having sex in public places before, and it wasn't like his own nocturnal activities were quiet as a convent. No, he could handle the sex. It was the scenes like the one going on in the kitchen right now that turned his grimace into a full-fledged frown.

Domestic bliss. Who would have ever thought the Bureau's Playboy of the Year would be jealous of domestic fricken bliss?

But you are.

And for that reason alone, he was considering going back into the bedroom where the beautiful blonde woman he'd picked up at the chief of police's birthday party was fast asleep, back to some sort of cowardly escape from the truth he'd been circulating around for the last six freaking months. Yeah, back to pretending none of this sucked and that he didn't have an easy way out sitting in his email inbox, waiting for a reply.

"Lucas, are you up?" Ev called him from the kitchen. *Shit, no hiding now. Coward. Goddamn coward.* He faced real, honest, dangerous situations every fucking day, faced down the worst of the city's underground crime syndicates and operations, looked over crime scenes with more regularity than a late-night police procedural on CBS, and he was fucking afraid to go into the kitchen in his own apartment. *Get it together, Vallejo.*

"I'm up, I'm up." He splashed water on his face, gave up on the smile and did a half-stumble down the hall from the bathroom into the kitchenette. They'd shared this apartment for almost three years, and though they hadn't managed to rearrange the furniture it had come with and were barely capable of keeping the refrigerator stocked, they'd gotten a handful of their early photographs together printed and framed — nothing fancy, but important memories nonetheless, memories that assaulted Lucas now.

The day they'd all finished training. *Dio, we were just freaking kids.* The day Ev had joined the BAU. The day Lucas had gotten his first bullet wound, smiling like an asshole in the hospital. The day Quinn had solved his first case — bioterrorism — and when they'd gotten rip-roaring drunk in celebration, he'd refused to let any of them eat anything because he was convinced it was poisoned.

For years, they had lived in these snapshots, friends. Best friends.

I don't know if I can anymore.

Ev thrust a large cup of coffee into his hands. "We're out of milk," she said without preamble. "Thought we could grab more fuel on the way to the airport."

"Airport?"

"Jesus, Lucas, don't tell me you forgot?" Behind her, Quinn snorted and Lucas only raised half a lip in a lame attempt at a growl.

"Forgot what? Evvie, I just worked eighty hours in four days. Use small words."

"Boss. Wedding. Montana." She paused, widening her eyes with each word and distracting Lucas too much for them to sink in. Or maybe it was just the set of her still-swollen lips, the way her long dark hair, usually tied up tight, looked messy and unkempt and sexy as hell, the way her skin glowed golden. Until. Until…

"Oh shit, that's today?"

"Yeah, hoss, that's today," Quinn said, turning away from the cabinet with the treasure he'd clearly been searching for, an unopened box of protein bars. Jesus, weren't they a pretty fucking picture? Capable of saving the world but, between the three of them, not capable of staying fed.

You'd probably starve to death on your own. And yet, he still hadn't turned down the fucking email from the Los Angeles Bureau… *Because you can't stand to see this every fucking day. Coward.*

Seemed to be the theme of the morning.

"How fast can you get packed?" Ev asked him, clearly unaware of the deep battle raging inside him. "I called a car for eight-thirty." She glanced at her watch then back at him. "How fast can you be packed and *showered*? Jesus, you smell like a dive bar."

This time he did manage a growl, which made her smile. God, she had a fucking smile. Ev played the part well, stiff, tight, buttoned to the chin. It was how she did her job day in and day out. But he knew the woman beneath the hard outer shell, knew her humor and kindness and the passion that drove her to do one real son-of-a-bitch job. Not that he and Quinn didn't have son-of-a-bitch jobs. They did, but getting inside the mind of serial killers and serial rapists? Give him good old-fashioned gang violence any day.

Before he could respond to her, though, there was a shuffle down the hallway and Carla or Cleo or whomever steadied herself against the wall to yank a heel on, before striding toward them.

She bristled a little when she passed the three of them, squared her shoulders and smiled at Lucas with her best *bravada*. It was good. He'd seen enough to know.

"Thanks for a fun night, Logan," she said, then pulled her bag over her shoulder and strode to the door, like she wasn't wearing a cocktail gown and those four-inch fuck-me heels at seven in the morning.

"It's actually…"

But the door slammed shut and he just sighed into the bathtub of coffee in his hands.

"How?"

"*When?*"

When he looked up, Quinn and Ev were both staring at him with raised eyebrows. They didn't look anything alike, not in skin tone or facial features, but their faces were so similar and humorous that if he had managed to get any of the scalding coffee into his mouth, he would have done a spit-take worthy of any late-night sitcom.

"I went to the party with the team last night," he said, purposefully turning away from both knowing expressions. Not like they hadn't been privy to his long and varied string of lovers over the years, but now that he could pinpoint the reason why he'd been bringing home passionate, intelligent, *forgettable* women on the nights he actually left the office, Lucas didn't feel all too inclined to talk about it.

"Jesus, when did you get home?" Quinn asked.

"Early enough for a quick romp," Lucas replied. "At least we made it to the bed." He shot Ev one of those salacious winks that anyone who knew him less would have mistaken for the real thing. Instead, she simply put her hands on his shoulders to turn him around and gave a light shove.

"Pack, shower, now," she ordered. "Don't come out until you're done."

Lucas scowled, but did as he was told, marching his sorry ass back down the hallway and toward the bathroom, wondering how in the hell he could have forgotten they were headed to Montana for Sam's wedding. *Gee, maybe it's the working yourself to the bone so you're too tired to face the truth stunt you're pulling? Nah, can't be.*

One problem at a time. For now, the most pressing was that he didn't have a clue when he had last done his laundry.

* * * *

From above, Montana looked like…trees. The few times he'd flown home to see his mom and sisters in

Cleveland, Quinn had watched the puzzle pieces of farmland turn to suburbs, then urban sprawl and finally city proper and he'd wondered how anyone in their right mind could stand to live so far from civilization. Sure, it took him half a fucking day to get anywhere in the city when the president's motorcade was out, but still. DC, like Cleveland, was full of the hustle and bustle of life he would never grow tired of.

Especially since he knew how quiet the world could be at night.

He glanced out of the window again and absently stroked Ev's hair. She rarely wore her hair down, usually securing it in one of those schoolmarm buns that made her soft features look sharp and severe. He got it, of course he did. They all had their shields, external and internal, to get them through the jobs they did every day.

But that didn't mean he didn't enjoy playing with her loose dark curls while she slept on his shoulder. Her head was bent at one hell of an angle, but she'd been gone for over a week on a case involving a string of serial murders in upstate New York, and he figured she hadn't gotten a good night's sleep since she had left. She wasn't going to get it now. They were nearly in Helena, from where they'd rent a car and drive the couple of hours to Wolf Creek, a town no one had ever heard of, to spend a few nights enjoying the undoubtedly rowdy nuptials of two of their former trainers-turned-friends.

Good. Let someone else deal with the terrorists and the serial killers and the gang wars for a few days. The three of them hadn't really been away from work since the first days they'd started, and if that didn't make him feel tired down to his bones, nothing would.

Still, Quinn knew tired. And now, at least, he didn't sleep enough because he worked too hard, not because he spent his nights staring up at the ceiling, eyes dry and unblinking, memories plaguing him every time he closed them.

Yeah, he knew exactly how quiet the world could be at night, when the winds settled sand dunes and the rapid fire of machine guns disappeared to another village, another town, another impending tragic vignette. Sometimes, he didn't know if the wars he fought from his office at the FBI headquarters were easier or harder than all those nights he'd spent in the trenches, wondering if maybe the world was so quiet because his damned soul was resting for all eternity.

Ev's soft breathing dragged him from the thought in an instant, as it had done so many times in the past. With her holding him through the night, the nightmares of memories had lessened, stilling, giving him respite. She had brought him back from a place he'd sometimes worried he'd never return from.

And for that reason, and so many more, he loved her fiercely. It was the kind of intense emotion that scared the daylights out of him, made him wonder when and where he'd gone so off the path he'd expected of himself. He'd never planned to marry. Most special agents, in any division, were married to the job. Ev, more than he or Lucas, was out of town a lot, but with his hours and hers, they saw each other only a few times a week, if they were lucky. Still, dating someone who knew the FBI life was a sight easier than trying to date someone who didn't get it. He knew that from first-hand experience and the string of short-term lovers who didn't understand why they couldn't grab him for a cup of coffee during the day or plan a date a whole week in advance.

Ev got that. She got a hell of a lot more too.

And yet, though it was her job to do the psychoanalysis, he hadn't been able to shake the sensation that something was bothering her. It wasn't the job. He knew full well what that kind of wear and tear looked like on her face. But where he'd always been able to read her, for the first time since knowing her, Quinn felt as though something was missing. Or rather, *he* was missing something.

And, Jesus, if that didn't carve a hole in his chest made of fear more potent than anything caused by a goddamn terrorist threat.

He'd do anything for this wild woman, draped across his lap now. *Anything.* But though he spent his days at the helm of a special team of trained operatives, and though his life ran in strict, regular, perfect organization, the lack of control he felt now absolutely stemmed from the fact that he didn't know what that *anything* was.

The captain announced their descent and Quinn shifted, running his hands through Ev's hair to wake her without too much fuss. She came awake slow at first, then in an instant. Old habits died hard.

"Just headed to Montana," he said, his voice low and calm. Lord only knew how many times he'd woken like that, wondering how in the hell he'd gotten somewhere and how long he'd been asleep for. Side effect of the job.

She nuzzled in closer and it made his heart just a little tighter in his chest. This *cutesy* thing, this lovey-dovey PDA on an airplane thing — he'd never thought he'd be caught dead doing anything like it. Sure, he'd grown up with love. His parents had loved each other up until the day his dad's illness had taken over, when Quinn had been fourteen. And his mama still loved his dad to this very day. And both his sisters, pains in the ass though they had been growing up, were so, so important to him. But what he felt for Ev was a whole new ball game.

"Can you drive?" she murmured, finally sitting up and rubbing her eyes. They were a little red and puffy from the dry air and he fished a small bottle of drops from his pocket and handed it to her.

"Thank God. My contacts feel like sandpaper," she said, giving him a smile that made him hot and bothered in both the chest and the groin.

"Nerd." He shot her a wink. "And yeah, I can drive. I was able to sleep before you got in last night." Not that he ever slept as well without her.

"You guys are boring." Lucas popped his head up over the seat behind them and they both turned to face him. Lucas looked young. *Really* young. He was a few years below both Quinn and Ev, but not *that* many. Still, mussed hair, long enough to reach his shoulders now, two-day-old stubble and a wicked light in his dark-brown eyes made Lucas Vallejo look about twenty-five, on the high end. No matter, even if he did look and sometimes act like the arrogant playboy he'd been when they first met, Lucas was by far one of the best agents in the Gangs and Violent Crimes task force he ran, if not in the whole damn city. He, like Ev—even, Quinn had to suppose, like himself—used his outer shell, his pretty-boy looks and easy-going demeanor to get as far as he had all these years. Hell, they'd all had to sculpt their masks.

"You seemed to do a fine job entertaining yourself last night," Ev shot back, but the sting was vastly lessened by the wide yawn that cut through it. She pursed her lips. "No one said you had to talk to us."

"I don't have anyone else to talk to." He indicated to the empty seat beside him. "I'd take dentist chat over watching how totally domesticated you two are. God, it's like I don't even know you." He grinned. "Hey, Ev, remember the time you went home with the SEAL, what was his nickname, oh yeah, *Mr. Rocketlauncher,* and it wasn't because of his finesse with weapons."

She lobbed a crumpled napkin at him and hit her target square on. Quinn couldn't suppress a laugh, not when Lucas started laughing or when Ev's lips curved into a smirk. He'd needed this, after the week he'd had. Coming home to Ev and Lucas had been a staple of his life at the Bureau and he knew he couldn't survive a day without them.

"Dunno what you find so funny, Mr. Macho," Lucas said, insolent grin spreading. "I sure as hell wouldn't be smiling if I'd brought home my boss's daughter. Did you think of him while you were in bed?" Lobbing another napkin at Lucas' face seemed like a great idea, but the plane began its final descent and they turned away from Lucas to fasten their seatbelts.

The landing was smooth and, in a few minutes, they'd made it through baggage claim and toward the car rental. Then they were on the road, Quinn at the wheel, Lucas in the seat beside him and Ev stretched out in the back, fast asleep.

"This case really got to her," Lucas said quietly, once they were on the road. Quinn had never been to Montana, and the vast stretches of empty highway surrounded by farms and fields had a calming effect on his harried thoughts. He glanced away from the road to look at Lucas.

"Yeah, I thought so too." She'd called them from her motel room twice, while in Freemont, New York, and she hadn't done all that great a job convincing them she was fine. But that was Ev. She could put on her robot face with the best of them, but deep down she was the kindest, most feeling woman he'd ever met. And even if she had been a robot, child serial killers would have been rough on the soul.

"Let's give her a damn good weekend, Luc, what do you say?" Quinn asked. Lucas' face curved into a smile.

"A case-by-case weekend?" he asked with that boyish enthusiasm and, *God*, Quinn felt old. Back when they'd first gotten started, Ev at the Behavioral Analysis Unit, Quinn with Counterterrorism and Lucas in Gang Crimes, a division of the Violent Crimes Department, they'd had one hell of a tradition. When one of them got a really bad case, like shit the bed, goat-fuckery, FUBAR bad, they'd have a case-by-case night, where they'd share a case of beer, a twelve-, twenty-four- or thirty-six-pack, depending on the severity of the case. They'd been young and capable of bouncing back from some riotous hangovers, and the memories of those early years made Quinn smile.

"Why the fuck not?" he said. "Though if Sam's got an open bar, and I damn well hope she does with her salary, I'm going for more than cheap beer."

"Sounds like a plan," Lucas agreed. "I think we all need a chance to wind down. Ev most of all." He grinned at Quinn. "Let's make this a weekend we'll never forget."

Chapter Three

The Triple Diamond Ranch was gorgeous. There was no other way to put it. Ev had slept the three hours from the airport and so stumbled from the car, finally feeling awake for the first time in days, only to catch sight of the sprawling, incredible mountain range cutting across the gray sky. Even with the trees bare and the harsh bite of winter catching in every breath she took, Ev couldn't deny the beauty all around her.

They walked a short way up the path to the check-in office. It was warm inside and, after a moment, a striking, tall woman emerged from a back room. She started at them then smiled.

"Welcome to Triple Diamond!" she said. "I'm Lily Hollis. This is my sister Maddy's ranch and B&B. You're here for the Pierce-Hawkins wedding, right?"

Ev stepped between Quinn and Lucas and fished through her purse for her wallet. "We are," she said, handing over her credit card, and Lily Hollis tapped out a few keys on the computer before her.

"You're going to love the setup," Lily gushed. "Maddy's working on the barn right now—it's gorgeous! And so are the brides." She shot Ev a conspiratorial wink. "I used to do flower arrangements for weddings, so Sam asked me to make her corsage. There won't be a dry eye on Sunday, let me tell you."

Ev blinked in surprise. "I must admit," she said, "I thought there'd be more backlash about having a gay wedding out here."

Lily only laughed. "Wolf Creek is a lot more open-minded than you'd think," she said. "For instance, Maddy and I, well, we both have pretty unconventional relationships, ourselves."

Curiosity way, *way* piqued, Ev went to go ask exactly what that meant, but the door swung open, bringing in a burst of cold air and her former trainer at Quantico, Samantha Hawkins.

"You guys are late," she said, before rushing in to hug first Lucas, then Quinn then Ev herself, her blonde hair flying free from the back of the parka when her hood fell down. "Look at you, all grown up." She punched Quinn in the stomach and he wrapped one thick arm around her neck.

"Still taller than you, Sammy," he said. "And you should be happy we got our sorry asses out here at all. Ev didn't get in until three and Lucas apparently thought your wedding was *next* month."

Sam raised a brow and Lucas held up his hands in surrender. "Do I know anything?" he asked, eyes glinting in mischief. God, he was so fucking cute when he was up to something. *For someone else.*

"Go drop off your stuff and come meet us down in the restaurant," Sam said. "Aims is going to be so happy to see you. And everyone else is here, too, so make it quick."

Ev couldn't help but smile when Sam dashed off back out into the cold. She was a fairly small woman, but stuffed into her bright white parka, she looked a little like a happy marshmallow. Still, she was in love.

"Ah, you're our threesome," Lily said. Ev's heart stopped for a moment. Just a moment. Of course, they were a threesome. They'd even done the cliché and called themselves the Three Musketeers for a spell. They had always, always been a threesome. And yet there was something in Lily's voice that made the word seem heavy, loaded somehow, as if it were Ev's own subconscious saying it instead.

"Ha, yeah, we booked late," Ev said, her voice perfectly normal, thanks.

Lily waved her off. "No worries! Will you be wanting an extra bed brought in or..."

Does she know? No. There's nothing to know. But...

"Two beds, please," Ev said quickly. Even quicker, she covered it up with a joke. "Quinn kicks and Lucas snores, so I'll never get any sleep if I don't have my own bed." Quinn rolled his eyes and Lucas shot her a stupidly seductive wink. Lily just tilted her head and didn't say a word, which felt a hell of a lot more damning than if she had.

The small guest cottage was, for lack of a better word, adorable. Lily chattered on as they made their way down the path, sharing that Maddy had inherited the ranch from her uncle almost a year earlier, and had begun turning it into a B&B within a season. The guest cottages, ten in all, Lily explained, were recent additions to the two-dozen rooms in Holmwood Manor. They didn't look it. In fact, when the group cleared the small hill, with the great mountains rising in the distance and the rustle of stark wind through the empty trees, Ev couldn't deny that those rustic little cottages, all wood and stone aesthetic, most definitely looked like they belonged.

As they took the path down the hill, a man approached them. He was tall, almost as tall as Quinn, with dark-blond hair and a dazzling smile. The second he spied Lily in their small traveling crew, his face broke out into an enormous grin.

"Lils, I've been looking for you."

Lily stopped them and gave the man a smile.

"I was working the desk for Maddy." She turned to them to explain, "This is our biggest wedding yet so my sister called in the extra help. Dec and…" She paused. "We actually live in a cabin up the mountain. Dec and his partner Micah own the Black Reef Survival Camp."

"I knew you looked familiar," Quinn said, reaching out his hand to shake Dec's. "Quinn Langston. Did you teach a class in Houston maybe two years back?"

Dec nodded. "Yeah, we do some traveling classes." He paused for a moment. "You guys must be with the Bureau, then."

They nodded.

"Lucas Vallejo," Lucas said, shaking the man's hand, too.

Dec turned his smile to her, and Ev's whole body flushed. He *was* handsome. But she knew Lucas' pretty-boy, playboy tendencies more than well enough to know that a smile like that was never a good sign.

"Ev Monteiro," she introduced herself with a smile. "Nice to meet you."

"Dec McCormick. Welcome to Triple Diamond," he said. "Won't be nearly as exciting here as it is in DC, but I'm sure you'll have fun."

"I don't want exciting," Ev said. "We get enough exciting."

"Dec and Micah also work S&R," Lily explained, her voice holding a note of pride. "And I'd say it gets pretty exciting here on occasion."

There was that tone in her voice again and Ev couldn't shake the feeling that maybe she was missing something. Something she found herself more and more curious to learn about.

"Don't say those kinds of things in front of the guests..." Dec murmured under his breath, loud enough for the lot of them to hear. Lily turned a brilliant shade of pink that had nothing at all to do with the frigid winter air.

"Dec." She eyeballed him. "Also, you looking for these?" She dangled a set of keys in front of his face, and instead of responding, he just...kissed her.

Wow. That was one hell of a kiss. Ev had never *thought* she was into the idea of watching another couple kiss but...

"And here I thought we'd need to buy tickets to the show," Lucas said, when Lily and Dec finally broke apart.

He shot Lucas a wink. *Good, give the guy a taste of his own medicine.* Not that Lucas was gay. She'd wondered, when they had first met, but it was more a Latin flair than a desire to pick up and start sucking cock.

And maybe she was having altitude adjustment issues, because *wow, that was crude.*

"Go give the keys to Micah so I can show these three to their cottage." Lily's voice was filled with way too much humor — and lust — to be a command.

Dammit, this time Ev *knew* she wasn't imagining the look in Dec's eyes at Lily's words. *What the hell am I missing here?* Working for the Behavioral Analysis Unit hadn't come with a warning that she would psychoanalyze nearly every person that came her way, but there was definitely, *definitely* something between Lily and Dec that she was missing. The only question was *what*.

But Dec moved on and Lily continued to chatter about the ranch until they arrived at guest cabin number four. She handed them the keys and gave a friendly wave before heading back the way she had come.

The cabin was sparsely decorated but very cute. In one corner of the living room and kitchenette, a small fireplace took up most of the wall, with stacks of thick wood in a basket to the side. Down the hall, a door led into one of the bedrooms, housing a bed nearly as large as the room itself. Small, rustic touches, like a basket of flannel throw blankets, dotted the cabin, but the most spectacular was a large picture window framing the stark, stunning view of the mountains in the gray sky. Even though the cabin was pleasantly warm, there was an undeniable scent of snow on the air.

"Did you guys pick up on any vibes from Lily and Dec?" she asked, tossing her duffel onto the bed and rifling through it. The door was open, so her voice would carry down the hall, she realized.

"Yeah, hot ones," Lucas replied. Out of the corner of her eye, she watched him muss up his long hair, and a thrill ran through her. She'd touched his hair, of course, once when he'd broken his wrist and couldn't wash it himself and another time when he was too drunk to get a piece of bubble gum out of the end. Both hazards of the job. Still, her sudden desire to run her hands through his hair now was both unexpected and unwelcome.

"Never took you for a voyeur, Luc," Ev replied. She gripped the sweater she was looking for, pulled it free from the bottom of her bag, her movements jerky.

Behind her, she felt Quinn's warm presence, and a moment later he was kissing her ear gently.

"Did you ever analyze me for a voyeur?" he asked, his hard body pressing against her back and her ass and...*oh, baby.*

"I hadn't," she said, her voice just a little breathy. "But I've been wrong in the past. I suppose we'll just have to do a series of tests to find out."

"Studious little scientist," Quinn murmured against her ear. "Talk nerdy to me, Dr. Monteiro."

She tried to laugh, but the sound came out a little husky, and she turned around to face him, to kiss him, to touch him, her body suddenly craving the connection of Quinn's, only to stop when she caught sight of Lucas standing in the doorway to the bedroom, arms folded across his chest and a smug smirk on his face.

"You just called me a voyeur then proceeded to dry hump with the door open," he said.

God, the man had a beautiful voice, all rolling, lilting, bedroom tones. Seductive and rich, like honey upon her fingers. Quinn, on the other hand—who hadn't moved from his position, most likely because he was sporting a sizable erection now and it would be obvious the minute he stepped out from behind her—Quinn wasn't seductive at all. He was darkness and smoke and unbridled passion. He was just a little dangerous, both because he couldn't be easily analyzed and because he knew exactly what he did to her.

"I'm going to take a shower," Ev said, her voice way too cheery. "I'll meet you guys at the party, okay?"

Quinn and Lucas exchanged a look and Ev just shook her head. "Whatever perverted fantasies you two are coming up with right now, I can promise you I don't want to hear it."

But as she escaped into the bathroom to take the shower she hadn't planned on taking until that moment, Ev knew she wasn't running away from their fantasies at all, but rather her own.

Chapter Four

When Ev finally emerged from the shower, Quinn and Lucas were gone and that sent a wave of relief washing over her. *They're my best friends. I shouldn't be happy they're gone.* Except it was getting harder and harder to deny the desire Lucas inspired within her, and she was afraid if she acknowledged it, she'd have to acknowledge all the other sticky, dangerous parts that came with it.

But I love Quinn. And she did, with the whole of herself that knew if anything ever happened to him, she would be wretched. Still, even dead on her feet, she hadn't been able to fall into sleeps deep enough to ignore the dreams about Lucas that had plagued her over the last months, or the curiosity that stoked a decidedly non-scientific part of her brain into wondering about…about *both* of them.

But people didn't do that, so Ev pulled on her super-cozy cable-knit sweater she never got to wear because she was never home from work long enough to wear anything, yanked a beanie over her wet hair, pulled on her warmest coat and stepped out into the cold wind Even though they'd gone two hours west from DC, the sun, what little of it had been there when they arrived, had nearly disappeared, leaving a cool, gray-purple glow in its wake. The air was crisp and blistering, but it was a dry kind of cold and she simply let herself enjoy it. The path was softly lit by pretty golden lanterns and she headed past the other cabins, the main manor house—Holmwood, Lily Hollis had told her—and toward the cozy communal room where the group of them were probably all already deep into the hard liquor.

Fine. Not only was she not driving, she didn't have to be anywhere for days. Dammit, she wanted to get sloshed.

But before Ev made it to the small building, she heard a noise coming from the toolshed behind Holmwood Manor. Instincts on high alert, she reached for her handgun, only to remember that it was safely stored in a lockbox back in the room. Still, she slunk around the building, body tense, heart moving slow and steady in her chest, as she peeked into the shed and…

It was Lily Hollis, held up against the wall with her pants on the ground and her legs wrapped around…

A man who was decidedly *not* Dec McCormick.

Ev hightailed it out of there faster than if there'd been a gun put to her head. When she arrived at the mess, she found Lucas and Quinn sharing a couch with Sam and her fiancée Aimee, and Aimee's sisters, Maya and Jodie. Others that Ev knew from the teams and their training were sharing the tables, the bar and a rug before the fireplace, happily digging into more than a few pitchers of cold beer and hot toddies.

"You go running or something?" Lucas asked when she came over to them. Ev must have looked confused because he added, "Your face is flushed, Evs."

She pulled off a glove and touched her face. It wasn't flushed — it was hot, burning against her icy fingers.

"Must be the cold," she managed. *Yeah right.* If her flush had been caused by anything other than embarrassment, she'd eat the glove in her hand.

Of course, it couldn't have anything at all to do with the curiosity and lust burning you up from the inside out, could it? Course not.

Rather than dwelling on it, Ev made her rounds through the small crowd, greeting old friends and being introduced to Aimee's and Sam's family members. She caught sight of a man whom she didn't recognize sitting alone at the bar, and turned to DC detective Cole Wicks.

"Who is that?" she asked, indicating the man as subtly as she could.

Cole narrowed his eyes.

"I think that's Sammy's brother, but I don't know for sure. I haven't seen him actually talk to anyone."

That's odd. I didn't know Sam had a brother.

Before she think any further on it, the door opened and Lily Hollis stepped in. She glanced around the room and spotted Ev and, for a moment, Ev actually felt nervous. *Nervous? Why the hell would I feel nervous?* This woman whom she had known barely an hour was perfectly allowed to keep her own business, and it didn't matter at all that Ev had accidentally walked in on her…

Getting fucked hard and fast against the wall?

Psh, it wasn't as though Ev's sex life was lacking for anything. Still, Lily's eyes were imploring, even across the room, so Ev grabbed her jacket and slipped through the crowd to join Lily outside. Lily Hollis was really beautiful, even dressed in all her layers of puffy winter attire, her long brown hair tucked into loose braids under an equally puffy hat.

"Do you mind going for a walk?" Lily asked. "I think I should clear some things up."

Ev didn't hesitate. Ever since she'd met this woman, she'd wondered if she was missing part of the puzzle, and her curiosity won out in an instant.

Lily led them a short way from the house, until they came to a clearing at the top of the hill. There was a small bench overlooking the purple-gray valley below, and they settled before the peaceful vista.

"I'm not cheating on Dec."

Well, that's a bold way to start.

Lily laughed, clearly coming to the same conclusion. "I'm just...I'm sure that was your first thought, so I wanted to clear things up."

Which, of course, only makes them murkier.

"So?" Ev wracked her brain for some kind of explanation, but she couldn't find a single one that would fit into the scenes she had witnessed this afternoon.

"The man you saw me with," Lily began, "that's Micah, Micah Ellison. See, I have sort of an unusual relationship."

Then Ev realized there was only one explanation and...*shit.* Because she'd just been using that as the last strong pillar in her defenses and now she had one hell of a wrench in the works.

"You're dating both of them," she said quietly. "And they know."

Lily smiled. "They definitely know. Dec and Micah have been friends a very long time and we stumbled for a while, but now we're really happy." She turned to face Ev, and her expression held no secrets or hidden agendas, only warmth and understanding. "I see now that I jumped to conclusions about your relationship with the two men you came here with," she said. "Just thought I'd let you know why."

Ev was silent a long moment. *This is crazy. People don't do this. People don't date two straight men at the same time.*

And yet, the expression on Lily's face now, contentment and ease, and the joy she'd seen in Dec McCormick's eyes when he had first caught sight of Lily on the path, those were raw emotions, ones that couldn't be faked. And lord only knew she saw enough of the depravity of humans all the time. Maybe just this one time, thinking outside the box didn't have to be a terrible thing.

For someone else.

"How?" It was the only question that could sum up the madness of the whole idea succinctly.

"It's simpler than you think," Lily said, shrugging. "My sister Maddy, who owns this place, she beat me to the punch. When I saw how happy she was with her husbands, I don't know, I fought it for a while. It's not an easy thing to wrap your head around, but Maddy was really happy and I figured if that was what it took, well, damn, I wasn't gonna judge."

They stared out at the vista, low, thick clouds rolling through the valley. It was definitely going to snow, and soon. The wedding itself was scheduled for the day after next, so she hoped it held off until then.

"I'm not advocating for this," Lily said quietly. "I understand you're dating Quinn and he's *hot*. Damn, woman, good for you. But it seemed like you should know there's more than one way to skin a cat."

Ev winced but smiled through it. "Not a sexy image," she replied. "And I'm not... Quinn and I are happy."

They were. *She* was. And yet... Yeah, always an *and yet.*

Instead of focusing on that, she changed the subject. "You're pretty good at reading people, Lily," she said. "Most people don't see past the mask and I've worked hard to keep it that way."

This time, Lily Hollis' pretty smile was sad and Ev cocked her head, waiting patiently for Lily's story. Sometimes patience, time, allowing someone the breath they needed to come to an answer all on their own — made or broke a case — or a relationship.

"I lost my fiancé when I was a senior in college," Lily said. "Cancer. I learned a thing or two about putting on a mask, Ev. And recently, about letting people see past it, too."

I let people see past my mask. I let Quinn and Lucas in. And isn't that telling, Miss Behavioral Analyst?

"Thank you for coming to find me," Ev said, when the silence between them stretched like the empty gray sky through the valleys. "I... I don't spend a lot of time with friends outside of work, and this is refreshing."

Lily gave her glove-covered hand a squeeze. "For me, too, Ev," she said, her smile genuine and happy now. "Come on, I'll introduce you to Micah and Maddy and her husbands."

They made their way back to the mess hall and Ev felt both more at ease and more confused than she had in a long time. They'd been in this alien land for barely a day, and already her understanding of what was up and what was down was wildly muddled. One thing was certain, however. Lily Hollis was happy, which meant that some version of the insane, crazed fantasy that had been circling Ev's mind for months was, if nothing else, *possible*. But as to what to do with the information, Ev didn't have a goddamn clue.

* * * *

Quinn's attention ping-ponged between the group of men sitting across from him and Lucas at the poker table. Most of the wedding party had found their way back to the cottages and rooms in the main house, and a couple of the locals had invited him and Lucas to play a few rounds in the back room of the mess hall. Since Ev had happily told them she'd spend the night with Sam and the others then turn in early, he and Lucas agreed. He'd folded on the first round of this new game and was now contenting himself with his beer and simply observing the world around him. Dec McCormick sat next to a large man who had introduced himself as Micah, also of the Black Reef Survival Camp, whom Quinn vaguely remembered from their workshop in Houston a few years back. Beside them were two of the Triple Diamond ranch managers and part-owners, Ryder Dean, who pretty much went open-call casting for country boy, and Christian Harlow, who wore his dark hair almost as long as Lucas did and, theylearned, rode a Harley.

The men were relaxed and at ease and even though he didn't have Ev's BAU training, Quinn couldn't help but think they were more than friends. He wasn't getting a gay vibe from any of them, simply an intimacy he didn't quite understand.

It's like how when Lucas and Ev and I hang out. And it turned out we weren't just friends, either. At least, he and Ev weren't. Though he'd seen Lucas' bare ass more times than a man needed to if he lived to be two hundred, Quinn had never felt the inkling of an urge to experiment. And yet...

So, feeling pleasantly buzzed on local beer and the knowledge that he could most sleep late tomorrow morning, he came right out and asked it.

"So, we met Lily, but do you guys have girlfriends, too?"

Lucas snorted and Quinn just shook his head. Lucas was forever on him about subtlety, but coming from a guy who eyebrow-waggled the panties off more women than most Washington politicians, the message fell a little flat.

For a minute, the card room was quiet. *Really* quiet. Like, *whoa did I just set off a bomb* quiet?

"Is no one else gonna take this one?" Ryder asked, glancing around at the rest of the men. He made a dramatic show of sighing then turned back to face Quinn and Lucas.

"In a sense, yeah, we have women in our lives. It's just a little unconventional."

Lucas leaned forward, obvious enthusiasm in his eyes. "Lay it on us," he said. Lucas had always been a sucker for scandal that wasn't his own.

"You met Lils?" Micah asked. They both nodded. "Well, she's my girlfriend, too."

Too. As in *also.* As in *with. Too,* as in Dec and Micah both knew the score full well and weren't just okay with it, but were willing to live their lives dating the same woman.

"And Madison Hollis?" Quinn asked slowly, still not quite able to wrap his head around the concept.

"Our wife," Ryder said on a grin. "As of July fourth. It's not legally binding, but we did a hand-fasting ceremony and we're working through some of the legal rights. What matters is that she's ours and we're not letting her go."

Beside him, Christian pushed his dark hair out of his face, which somehow made him look more fierce than less. "Damn straight, she is," he muttered, like he wasn't discussing the woman he loved.

"I knew it." Lucas' grin grew. "Lily kept hinting at something, I just couldn't figure out what."

"It works for us," Dec said, taking a long swig of beer. "I never thought it would, but it does. We almost lost Lily a few months ago, and it made us realize how much more important she was to us than doing things the way they've always been done, ya know?"

Quinn got it. He did. In a *that's for other people* sort of way. Because when his mind went to Ev, to her rare humor and the passion she threw into her job and the way she made his nightmares disappear, he felt a fierce possessiveness burning him right down to the soul. He couldn't even begin to imagine sharing her with another man.

Beside him, Lucas laughed at something one of the other men had said, and Quinn amended the statement. He'd been sharing her with Lucas, and Lucas with her, since the very beginning. It didn't get tighter than their relationship. And yet, of course, he couldn't *share* her with Lucas, not that he had any idea if that was even what she wanted.

She has been off lately. Maybe all she needs is a change of pace.

And before Quinn could get a goddamned grip on himself, his mind began to whirl with images of Ev and Lucas on the bed in their little cottage, of watching his two best friends taste and lick and suck, of feeling her wrap her plush lips around his cock while Lucas...

"Well, good for you," he said, not feeling even a little of the nonchalance that he threw into his voice. "Can't be easy for you guys."

"Can't be easy for you, either," Micah replied. "I'll be honest, I think more people are bothered by the whole interracial relationship element of this than the two-boyfriends part." He indicated his dark skin, Native American, from the Blackfeet Nation, he had explained, and, when he laughed, it felt to Quinn like the whole room shook. Micah Ellison was one big dude. "How fucked up is that?"

Quinn grimaced his agreement and lifted his beer up in solidarity. They'd experienced a few instances — raw as epithets hurled across the street, subtle as the looks they got from waiters — but Quinn didn't give a good goddamn. Ev was his and as long as she was happy, no one else mattered.

"So, like, do you guys ever...?" Lucas was about as subtle as a freight train when it came to getting information out of a man, and not a little bit drunk on local craft beer. "I mean, it's fine if you do... I'm just curious."

The truth was, though, Quinn was pretty curious himself. He'd been an early supporter of gay rights and considered himself an ally in a business that could go very strongly in the other direction. Military, Bureau — they'd both surprised him before. But, though he supported the LGBT community, he didn't have a gay bone in his body. Nor did he want a gay bone *in* his body. And if the idea now percolating dangerously close to his frontal lobe managed to stick, he needed to know the answer.

"Nah." Ryder dealt a new hand of cards. "I mean, listen, you're gonna see another dude's dick. It's just a thing. But ya get over it."

This was *so* weird. Of all the things Quinn could have ever expected of coming out to Montana for his boss's ranch wedding, it sure as Hades on ice wasn't this. *And yet you're intrigued. You're more intrigued than you want to admit to yourself.*

So instead of speaking or allowing his wandering thoughts to slam his brain any harder than they already were, Quinn leaned back in his chair and chugged the rest of his beer. Christian caught his eye and chuckled.

"It's a lot less complicated than it looks from the outside," he explained. "I mean, all right, for us at least. But we were sharing women before Maddy, in bed. So the transition wasn't that hard."

It was the word *sharing* and the dam broke in Quinn's mind, more of those raw, carnal images, Ev bent over the couch, her ass high in the air, Lucas pounding her from behind with an iron grip on her hips, holding her in place. To him.

Get your shit together, Langston. This isn't going to work.

Yeah, it's just the two examples of it working that have me all confused.

And ah, *fuck*, he was definitely confused. Even after the conversation turned away from their women, to universal male conversations of sports, to the comparison between Christian's Harley and Quinn's own vintage BMW bike that he rarely ever got to ride. Then, two by two, the other men bade good night and headed back to their women, likely to find creative and scintillating ways to stay warm in the blustering Montana mountains.

And damn it, no matter what Quinn did, he couldn't shake the urge to give Ev a warm-up just like it.

Chapter Five

Quinn Langston wasn't a man who let people in easily. Lucas had learned that from day one, right about the time he'd learned Evangeline Monteiro was not a woman to take lightly. But he'd known them both for years and, more pressingly, for the most important years, and one glance at Quinn right now told Lucas his best friend had something on his mind.

Or maybe you're getting paranoid because you have something on your mind. Maybe all that talk about sharing lovers got to you, Vallejo, ever think about that?

Thought about, *ha*. His full cock was straining against his jeans, wondering why he wasn't back at the cottage right now, taking Ev from behind while Quinn filled her mouth. The fantasies of filling Ev, of claiming her however he could, however she'd let him, weren't anything new. But the added and surprisingly easy element of Quinn was. After all, who wanted to fantasize about fucking the girl of his dreams with his best friend hanging around to watch? And yet they'd always been a unit, symbiotic and able to depend on one another without question. It only made sense Quinn would fit right into this too, dammit.

"So, I'll admit, I wasn't expecting that," Lucas said, looking down at his beer as though it was the most fascinating thing in the world. Getting Quinn to open up about anything required a certain light touch.

Quinn rolled his eyes. "You could say that again." He stood and headed into the main mess hall. "I think I need something stronger to drink before that conversation makes sense. Want anything?"

Lucas followed him to the small bar setup. In the grate, the blazing fire had burned down to embers, the sound drowned out by the blustering wind rattling the windows in their frames. *Oh, yeah, Montana's fucking cold.* It made DC winters look like a day at the kiddy ice rink. Though, of course, when he'd moved east from Los Angeles, that first December he'd thought he'd died and gone to a frozen-over hell.

You could always go back.

"Make it a double," Lucas said to Quinn, instead of replying to the insidious voice in his head, the one that kept reminding him of the job offer sitting in his inbox. He'd deal with it when he was back in Washington. Or maybe never.

"Could you imagine sharing a woman with another man?" Quinn asked, sipping long at his drink and, quite obviously to Lucas, covering his eyes. Though he did his damnedest to hide it, Quinn tended to give away everything with his eyes.

"I don't know," Lucas answered, the lie getting a little caught in his teeth, sticky and weighted. "I guess it depends on the woman." He shrugged. "And the man.

I mean, I don't think there's anyone else I'd trust enough, other than you."

Quinn considered this then slowly placed the whiskey glass down on the bar counter. His hands were a little unsteady, courtesy of the many beers they'd shared over poker. Of course, that was the only sign Quinn gave of being nearly sloshed. And he was. If he had too much more, Lucas would be carrying him back to the cabin, not that he was feeling walk-the-white-line-sober right then either.

"Yeah, man," Quinn replied quietly. "It'd have to be you, too."

They fell into an awkward sort of silence and Lucas didn't think it had anything to do with the admittedly erotic thoughts swirling in his mind — images, so many fucking goddamned images that he knew he had no right to but couldn't seem to hold at bay.

"Have you ever?" Quinn asked. "Been with another man in bed?"

Lucas shook his head. "Two women once. I know everyone jokes about it, but if they hadn't been into hooking up with each other, I honestly don't know how I would have handled it. It's a little overwhelming in the moment."

"Do you think she'd be overwhelmed?" Quinn's voice sounded a little raw, like he'd spat the question out before he could stop himself. There it was. Lucas hadn't been imagining anything about his friend's behavior and he wasn't even the behavioral analyst. Ten freaking points to Slytherin. But if Quinn wanted to ask something, he needed to ask it outright, no room for confusion. Because if he was about to ask what Lucas thought he was, there couldn't be any room at all for confusion.

"Who, Q?" he said quietly. In an instant, Quinn understood the rules of the game. *Well, hey, it's almost like we know each other or something.*

"I've seen the way you look at her," Quinn said, his voice low, almost apologetic. For what, Lucas didn't really want to analyze. "I know you find her as attractive as I do." *Attractive* was like calling the Pope *spiritual. Attractive* was like calling Michelangelo a cartoonist. Attractive didn't even begin to cover the myriad ways Lucas ached for her touch, and Quinn obviously knew that.

"You know I do," Lucas said honestly. "She's pretty damn incredible."

Quinn pulled two shot glasses out from behind the counter and filled them both to the brim. "Drink," he ordered.

Curious, and always intrigued when Quinn Langston began to lose control, Lucas tipped his head back and downed the shot. *Shit*, the stuff burned, but he did feel a lot warmer after it went down. Quinn filled it back up again and Lucas raised an eyebrow. But his friend didn't say anything, just knocked the full shot glass to Lucas' and downed his second one. So Lucas followed suit, an odd sense of anticipation rioting through him.

"I want to offer Ev a threesome." This was said way too quickly, and to the odd effect of Quinn tripping over some of the syllables. Mr. Controlled Military Man was definitely feeling a fit of nerves.

That apparently Lucas was adding to by not replying, because Quinn started talking again, getting faster as he went. "I just feel like something's been on her mind and I want to change up the pace, ya know, distract her from work and everything for a while, and you're the only person in the world I could ever imagine doing anything like that with and shit, man, interrupt me, for fuck's sake."

"Are you sure?" They weren't the first words Lucas would have thought he'd say, not when Quinn was handing his fantasy to him on a silver platter. But he'd been around the block enough times to know that when things got messy, they got *really* messy and the last people in the whole damn world he wanted messy with were Quinn and Ev.

Or rather, messier. Because there was no way this wasn't going to be hard — more, and wasn't it a hell of a time for a bad pun? But the second he touched her, Lucas knew he was going to have to acknowledge some pretty difficult truths.

"Yeah I'm sure. I'll be honest, listening to those guys got me curious. I mean, *curious*, ya know?" Yeah, the evidence of exactly how much Lucas *knew* was straining against his zipper right then. "And I don't know, we promised each other we'd give her a good time, right? Case-by-case weekend?"

Lucas couldn't help but laugh. "We did promise."

Quinn sobered. "Shit, man, if I'm way off base here, tell me. We could just end the conversation and never talk about it again."

But it wouldn't be so easy. Because Lucas knew that whatever this was, that whatever his lifelong love and affection for these two people were, whatever his desire was, this could only end in chaos — for him, at least. And he knew with equal certainty that he couldn't possibly walk away.

"Nah, you're not off base." He poured himself a little more whiskey and sipped at it this time. "I just want to be sure you won't regret asking me in the morning."

Quinn shook his head. "I know I won't," he said, his voice that commanding tone that worked so well in the office.

"So, what, are we going to ask her or...?" And what was the schedule on the whole seduction thing, because he might need about twenty minutes in a cold shower if nothing was planned for tonight.

"I think we should seduce her," Quinn admitted, his light brown skin actually flushing at the word. "I mean, just to make it exciting and interesting, less clinical, ya know? And there's the party tomorrow night."

Quinn made some excellent points.

"Well then," Lucas filled the shot glasses again, holding them up for celebration rather than courage this time. "I look forward to the best case-by-case weekend yet."

Even if it was the stupidest thing he'd ever do.

Chapter Six

Ev woke to a hard heat pressed against her ass. The bed was warm and cozy and soft and if she never had to get up to brave the world outside, she'd die happy. She snuggled back against the pressure and became a little more conscious when said pressure jerked against her bare skin. So she snuggled again, and this time became fully aware of not only warmth, but the strong arms wrapped around her belly and the powerful legs tangling in hers.

"I'd stop moving that sweet ass if I were you, baby," Quinn growled against her ear. But in the warm, delicious comfort of his arms, her desire most definitely piqued with every evidence of Quinn's arousal, Ev was feeling playful.

"Or what?" she teased, pressing back into him with more intent in her motions this time.

"Or I'll turn it red for insubordination."

Now that's a thought. A really heady, sexy, intense thought that made her pussy quiver in demand, made

Ev want to press her panties to the side and slide herself down, sheathing her body completely over Quinn's cock. She'd never get enough of the feeling of him inside her, and she'd been fast asleep by the time the men had come down from the mess hall, undoubtedly wasted, the night before. But instead of thinking about the party or Lily and Maddy Hollis, whom she'd gotten to know, or Sam and Aimee, who were so blissed-out in love they looked like different people, Ev thought about the fastest way to get Quinn Langston's hard, hot dick inside her.

"I can hear the gears turning in your head," Quinn whispered in her ear. "And I'd much prefer you not thinking at all." Then, blessedly, he pushed her panties flush with one thigh, the position tight, with the way they lay spooned together on their sides, even tighter when he edged her wet pussy with one large finger then slowly, *God, slow enough to fucking kill*, pushed inside.

Of course, one finger wasn't nearly enough to bring about the pressure Ev so desperately needed, and she arched against his touch, grinding into his palm. He murmured the sweetest, most sinful, most delicious words in her ear, biting the lobe and the skin of her neck in between filthy promises.

'I'm going to make you beg for my cock, baby. God, you're so fucking wet. I can't wait to taste you on my fingers, to make you come until you're boneless in my arms then make you do it again.'

They'd never gone full scene, but Ev had long suspected Quinn had a bit of a Dom personality about him. Still, when she saw her lover every few weeks, sometimes only for an hour or two at a time, even vanilla sex didn't get boring.

"Jesus, I'm begging." Her words came out, desperate, husky and raw. "Quinn, please…" It seemed like she begged for his cock an awful lot.

"Not good enough." He continued his slow ministrations, sliding two fingers in and out of her pussy, and brought his other hand up to circle one peaked nipple, before he rolled it to a stiff point between his brusque fingers. "You're so ripe," he growled. "Juicy and sweet and delicious." His hand came around and cupped her whole breast in a shockingly possessive move and she nearly shouted, grasping the sheets as though they might somehow steady her in the whirling madness. Of course, the very thing that made her the craziest was also her rock, her port in the storm.

"*Quinn…*"

He shifted so the slick head of his cock was right at the entrance to her pussy.

"Tell me how much you want it," he demanded, teasing his plump crown against her hole. *Fuck.*

"I want it. Jesus, Quinn, I want it."

"More, Ev. You can do better."

She surged, his demanding tone making her mount higher, sending shards of lightning-white heat racing through her.

"Jesus *fuck*, Quinn. Stuff your cock in my cunt hole and fuck me like you mean it before I take things into my own hands." And just to prove she wasn't bluffing, Ev snaked her hand down her belly and toward her throbbing clit. Quinn caught her wrist before she could get any of the pressure she needed and, keeping her pinned to the bed, sank inch by ever-fucking-loving inch into her willing pussy.

She shattered, right then and there, the pressure of Quinn's hard erection stretching her, filling her, making everything but the sensation of him deep inside fall away as she rode the insane wave of pleasure.

"Yes, baby, give me your release. God, you're so tight." The control was nearly gone, threatening to fray with each press of those thick inches deep inside her. She wanted to give it to him, wanted to clench and pulse around Quinn's rigid cock. She loved the sensation of shattering around him and with each stroke of his hardness, she neared her climax. *So close, so fucking close...*

Her senses were on such high alert that the sound in the living room made her freeze. They were under the blanket, but the door was open — way too open for them to be doing what they were doing, though of course that was more than a little of the reason her body tingled and her skin burned for more.

Still, from her position on the bed, she could see movement, see Lucas sitting down before the fireplace. He wore only loose-fitting flannel pajama bottoms and his eyes were focused on a manila folder in front of him. But if he looked up...

From Lucas' view, they could have just been spooning right? And yet...her face was flush, her lips so swollen...

Then he lifted his head and his gaze caught hers across the room.

Does he know? He has to know...

And yet, the idea that Lucas maybe *did* know, that he wasn't ignorant of the fact that Quinn had his cock buried deep in Ev's throbbing pussy, didn't turn her off. In fact, her breasts actually tingled and the heat in her belly bloomed into something far more potent and dangerous. The fact that he was bare from the waist up and lounging back in a lavish leather chair didn't help either. His chest was a deep gold and the lines of powerful muscles were dusted with hair as dark as the long locks spilling over his shoulders. Ev wasn't sure whether she'd rather bury her hands in his messy morning hair or lick him from neck to waist and back again.

Yup, officially fucked. In more ways than one.

"Evvie, come back to me," Quinn said, his voice husky with what could have passed for sleep, but Ev knew so much better. Then she barely knew anything at all, because Lucas was holding her gaze, steady, dark, unblinking, even when Quinn pulled away and slid a few inches out of her, then pushed back inside. Her grip on the sheets was ferocious and desperate, and Ev sank her teeth into her bottom lip in an attempt to keep her scream buried deep down. *This is wrong. People don't get turned on by getting fucked in front of their best friends.*

But Quinn continued his slow assault on her body, even as Lucas held her gaze. His look didn't give anything away, but he was a goddamned FBI agent and if he couldn't tell by the sheen of sweat on her brow and her swollen lips exactly what was going on, she'd think he was getting soft. But even at this distance, even through the partially opened door, Ev could tell there was nothing soft about him, not the hard planes of his chest, or the dark look in his eyes or the way his pants pulled to an obvious tent…

No. Absolutely not. She would not be the person who got fucked from behind while teasing her best friend in the other room, she would not. She tried to tear her eyes away from Lucas' obvious arousal but managed only to catch his gaze.

He pursed his lips, those full, plush lips, and gave an almost imperceptible shake of his head.

No? No, don't tell? No, don't turn away? No, *don't stop?*

How the hell could she possibly know? The only thing she knew was that she was burning up with pleasure, the sense of need and desperation rioting through her body as it never had before and it had nothing at all to do with the fact that she was getting hardcore fucked while having a silent communication with her voyeuristic best friend. A best friend whom she'd been dreaming about for months... *No, nothing at all.*

"Come with me, baby." Quinn's voice was a raw growl in her ear. "Don't think about anything else, just your body wrapping around my cock like you were meant for me."

Did Quinn *know?*

She didn't think he could see Lucas from his position behind her, but maybe Quinn somehow just knew and knew, also, that the exhibitionism of the whole thing was ravaging her body with the ultimate pleasure, because he sure as hell wasn't asking her to stop.

Lucas stood from the chair, never breaking eye contact. He stretched, showing rippling tattoos and long, lean muscles, power and grace, like a cat on the prowl.

Then he licked his lips.

Ev's mind shattered in that moment. She ground her teeth together, her thoughts exploded, her soul burst and wave after wave of mindless pleasure beat an untamable course through her whole body. She tried to temper it, tried to hide the fact that she was clearly losing herself to the pounding lust Quinn's delicious cock pushed her into time and again, but it was so hard to keep her mouth shut or her moans silent when Lucas looked at her like that, half-naked, promising, deadly.

Because all she could think about was how it might feel to invite Lucas into the bed beside her, to press her swollen lips to his while Quinn pounded her from behind. In this moment of pure, pleasure-filled insanity, Ev couldn't deny herself those desires, those dangerous, secret desires she had no right to indulge.

"Shhh, baby, you're okay." Quinn was murmuring soft and sweet against her neck and she turned to kiss him. Not exactly, not now that she'd acknowledged to herself just what it was that she wanted, not now that she knew it wasn't only Lucas, but the idea of Lucas and Quinn together, the idea of all three of them strengthening the bond that had formed years and milestones before. But what could she say? Certainly not that.

Instead, she pushed her damp hair from her eyes and tried to make her smile nonchalant and not a combination of terrified and bonelessly sated.

"Yeah," she managed. "I'm more than okay."

It somehow was and wasn't a lie all at the same time.

* * * *

"Did you guys know Sam had a brother?" They were back in the mess hall, cozied up at a table close to the roaring fire and digging into a delicious breakfast. A shower and two cups of fresh, rich coffee later, Ev had been able to get her head on straight about the whole situation. It was almost funny. She'd been so in the throes of her own erotic haze that her fantasies had been distorted and a little crazy. But sitting next to Quinn and Lucas now, with all three of them dressed and enjoying a meal like they'd done so many freaking times throughout their friendship, everything felt back to normal. She didn't have any fantasies of licking her best friend from neck to navel, nope.

Liar.

"Is he here?" Lucas asked, "I didn't think she had any family left."

For someone like Ev, who came from a family as large as the day was long, it seemed so remarkably sad Sam might not have anyone of her own, with the exception of the one brother who was sitting in the corner of the mess by himself. He wore a large overcoat, which wouldn't have been odd in and of itself, except the mess hall was warm and cozy, with fireplaces burning hot at both ends. He stared out of the window and didn't touch the food on his plate or move for several long moments.

"I guess he's her brother. Wicks told me so yesterday."

"I think his name is Zach," Quinn said. "At least, that's what I heard Sam call him yesterday. I could be wrong."

Ev's family had always been prone to being overdramatic. Her mother's convenient lack of hearing every time she spoke about Quinn was nothing compared to the parties, dinners and holidays that comprised too much food and yelling over the heads of at least a dozen younger cousins. She loved them and they loved her, and though they all drove her batty — and growing up with three siblings really did that — Ev couldn't for a second imagine life without them. Sam worked full-time in DC and traveled the country for training programs, so she couldn't have seen her brother very often. So why on earth was Zach moping around like he was desperate to be somewhere else?

"You have your look, babe," Quinn said from behind his cup of coffee.

Ev glared at him. "I do not."

"Evvie," Lucas scoffed. "You can't see your own face."

The look referred to the expression she made when she started analyzing a person. Working behavioral analysis on a crazy, round-the-clock schedule made it difficult to shut down the parts of her brain looking for tics, symptoms or other signs of a person's thoughts or plans. It wasn't always for psychopaths or killers. She'd found herself analyzing the behavior of friends, family and coworkers more times than she could count. Still, no one liked being caught red-handed. Instead, she stuck out her tongue.

"Aren't you supposed to be the mature one here?" Lucas asked, before sticking his tongue out right back at her.

"Aren't you supposed to be the mature one here?" Ev mocked, shaking her head from side to side.

Behind a copy of the local newspaper he'd picked up at the door to the mess, Quinn chuckled. "I think I've figured out who the mature one is," he said, his voice dry and all the funnier for it.

Ev glanced at Lucas, then, in unison, they both turned back to Quinn and mocked, *"I think I've figured out who the mature one is."*

He nearly choked on the sip of coffee he'd been taking and very dramatically lifted the paper higher so neither of them could see his face.

Ev glanced back over at Lucas. This was the way it was supposed to be. Friends, just friends. Whatever insane thoughts had passed through her head this morning during her lust-filled fog were nothing more than anomalies, products of her desperate pleasure Ev had no control over. She didn't want to lick Lucas, tousle his hair or kiss those always-swollen, pretty-boy lips. Not at all.

Liar.

Chapter Seven

Looking pretty was *hard*. Not only had she been wearing a uniform of comfortable slacks and sensible blazers for the better part of five years with little reprieve, but it was cold as a witch's tit outside, and Ev would be damned if she froze her cooch off from going outside in Montana in January in a fucking dress for the sake of fashion.

The guys, of course, could get away with a pair of nice jeans and the warm, cozy-looking sweaters that Ev was considering wearing one of as a dress over the pair of flannel leggings she was grateful to have packed last minute. At the moment, they were both mulling over suit options, which meant she'd have plenty of sweaters to steal from.

"How nice are we supposed to look?" she asked Quinn, when he came back into the bedroom, his few-day-old stubble shaved clean. She stared at her open suitcase.

"I think Aimee said cocktail," he told her. "But it's really cold and feels like snow."

Yup, nothing like wearing a cocktail dress in a blizzard.

"You think I can get away with wearing a sweater?" she asked. Quinn tried to smile, but his eyes glazed over and Ev rolled her own. "No help, no help at all. I need more women in my life."

Actually.

She grabbed her coat and headed for the door. "Be back in a few!"

It did feel like snow. The sky was gray and heavy and the telltale winter scent made her nostalgic for the days she and her siblings had spent home from school, torturing one another and their mother in turn. Still, the snow meant the air was a little warmer than it had been and Ev enjoyed the brisk walk.

It didn't take her long to find the Hollis sisters. Lily and Maddy were in the foyer at Holmwood, sharing hot chocolate and what looked to be a bottle of Irish cream liqueur on the table between them.

"I need help," Ev said, her breath coming out on a cold sigh, when she made her way into the warm room.

Maddy clapped her hands. "Trouble with men, clothes or mothers?" she asked. "I'm guessing men."

Lily grinned and waggled her eyebrows. "No way. Have you seen how those two look at her? It's definitely clothes." She looked at Ev with a smile on her face. "You didn't pack anything warm enough for Sam and Aimee's cocktail party, right?"

"You're a mind-reader," Ev said, her face breaking out into a smile. "I'm desperate. I tried to ask Quinn, but the big, scary military man gets all flustered when I ask for basic fashion advice."

"It doesn't get any better when there's two of them, let me tell you," Maddy Hollis said smiling. "Christian has very seriously recommended I start wearing motorcycle tanks to greet my guests." She stood and walked over to the small kitchenette at one side of the Holmwood foyer. "First things first." She ladled a steaming mug of hot cocoa from a pan on the stove and brought it back to the table, then proceeded to pour in a generous dose of Irish cream. "You gotta get warm. Then we'll go closet hunting."

Well, that sounded like a damn fine plan if Ev had ever heard one.

Ev actually had fun. She couldn't remember the last time she'd been so silly, so frivolous with her spare moments. The only people she really considered friends were Quinn and Lucas and the members of her eight-person team, with whom she spent most of her time. She loved her sisters and her brother, but when she made it home, it was usually a quick hop on a long journey, often only to be called back to work in an instant, and most of her friends from before she'd joined the Bureau didn't get her lifestyle, or why she wasn't around for coffee during the afternoon or drinks on a Friday night. Of course, she considered Sam and Aimee close friends, and there were others, Ev was sure of it, but unless they worked in the world of the FBI, they couldn't understand, and most people in her life didn't.

But in Madison Hollis' bedroom, in the house just down the path from Holmwood Manor, with the two Hollis sisters, all three of them a little tipsy on cream liqueur and Maddy tossing outfits at them from the cavernous closet, Ev was having fun. Genuine, feel-good, no-strings-attached fun.

"You bitch," Lily gasped. She was holding up a cozy-looking pink sweater, her mouth opened wide. "I have been looking for this for a month. You told me you didn't know where it was."

Maddy grinned and Ev tried not to laugh. It was a fight she'd indulged in with both her sisters plenty of times. Natalia was nearly ten years older than Ev, closer to a second mother growing up than an older sister, but she and Aurora, just one year, eight months, two weeks and three days older—not that Aurora ever let her forget it—had bickered about clothing, books, the cleanliness of their shared bedroom and the occasional pop star hottie who was most definitely in love with one of them. Being here with Lily and Maddy reminded Ev a whole hell of a lot of being at home, and she felt a sudden ache to be back in her mother's kitchen, surrounded by the people who loved her.

At least, *most* of the people who loved her. The man who loved her was currently a few guest cabins down the lane, probably still trying to decide if she had been kidding about wearing leggings to a cocktail party.

"Not in front of the guests!" Maddy said, but her voice was so full of giggles she could barely get the words out, even when Lily took the sweater back and marched over to the bed, grabbing the bottle off the dresser when she did.

"Okay, what's the weirdest guest you've ever had?" Ev asked. She was feeling relaxed, more at ease than she had been in a long time, especially when Lily handed the liquor bottle over without asking and she drank deep.

"Well, we've only been open since the summer," Maddy explained. "And the cabins are a new addition—your party is the first to use them, actually.

But the weirdest guest... Oh, there was a guy who brought his dog. Now, I love dogs, but this snappy little shit—he dressed it up in different costumes every day! And designer costumes too, I mean, he was spending a fortune on designer dog costumes..."

Ev blinked. "What was he doing out here?" she asked, curiosity piqued.

"Land developer or something. But it was clear who was the owner in that relationship." Maddy waved a hand and went back to digging in the closet.

Ev passed the bottle back to Lily. "Anyone you've come across?" she asked. Lily grinned.

"I don't actually work here," she said, eyes twinkling. "But yeah, there have been a couple. I have met a few cool people—one woman was a photographer for *National Geographic*. That was awesome. Another couple was doing a motorcycle trip across the country." Her smile turned into a thin line. "You know who does creep me out, though?" she asked. "There's a guy here now who gives off some weird vibes." She clamped her mouth shut. "And I'm being unprofessional, so shutting up now. Forget I said anything."

Ev shook her head. "It's Sam brother, right?"

Lily grimaced but nodded. "I think his name is Zachary or Zachariah. I don't know, I've never seen him talk to anyone but Sam, and only rarely. And they've been here nearly a week. I don't know. It's just a feeling."

Ev had been with the BAU for nearly five years. Some days, science won out. Some days her years of training and school and analysis were what led them to a killer. Other days, it was pure gut instinct.

"Never underestimate *just a feeling*," she said to Lily. "You'd be amazed at how many people are still alive because of their gut instinct." And Ev's gut, where Zachary-Zachariah Hawkins was concerned, was feeling a little twingy.

But she didn't want to think about that, not in this room with these wonderful women and one hell of a hot boyfriend who she had every plan of impressing at the party that night.

"Ooh, what about this?" Maddy's head was deep in the pile of sweaters at the far end of her closet and the question came out muffled. But then she turned around and held up a dark red dress that made Ev's face break into a smile. It was long-sleeved and velvet—thank God the trend was back in fashion—and curved down, probably coming to below her knees.

"Wear this with those black boots you've got," Maddy said, her voice the full co-conspirator of a woman on a mission to help a friend. "Your man is gonna drop his jaw when he sees you in it, let me say that."

Lily made a sound from the bed. She was sitting on top of her pink sweater and drinking more wine from the bottle, her smile wicked. It seemed as though the trait ran in the family.

"Not just one man, honey." Lily raised the wine in salute.

Ev shook her head. "I can see why you need two boyfriends to wrangle you," she said. "I don't think just one would be able to handle the job." It was meant to be a joke. Lily clearly took it for one, and a week ago Ev wouldn't have thought twice on it. But looking at the sisters now, happy as they were, *normal* as they were, horrible as that sounded, Ev wondered if maybe her flippancy was misplaced, if maybe her whole understanding of their dynamic was misunderstood.

Lily and Maddy Hollis didn't have two partners because they wanted the extra attention or love. They had two partners because they loved two men, and those men were able to see past the strictures of social norms to give the women that they loved what made them happiest.

What a fucking head-trip.

"Don't think too much on it," Maddy said. "Lily runs her mouth."

Lily stuck her tongue out at Maddy, and the women, Ev included, all laughed. But even while they teased her hair and tossed some new and different makeup her way, Ev didn't go back to that easy feeling she had enjoyed just a few minutes before.

Instead, her mind whirred and her thoughts chased one another—Quinn filling her up while Lucas watched, only this time Lucas knew it, and his eyes would flame dark and hot and Ev had to shake herself several times as she finalized her outfit and makeup and got ready to go and meet her boyfriend. Singular.

Right.

The party was in full swing by the time she made her way down from Maddy Hollis' house to the mess hall. The chairs and tables had been cleared away and the main room had been opened for a wide dance floor. They needed it, since she spotted many people who had only just arrived, others from the Bureau, a few she recognized from local precincts they had visited over the years. The beat was a slow, deep grind, and the dim lights and general pulsing of the room made Ev feel like she'd stepped out of the Montana ranch and back into the heart of DC club culture. She had to assume. She didn't have a lot of experience with DC club culture. *Or any club culture.*

And that was why she felt on edge, that and nothing else. Certainly not the small seeds of doubt taking root in her mind, or the curiosity, the wonder, the ache deep in her belly to know if there was something more out there.

She grabbed the wedding's signature cocktail, a winter wonderland martini, and downed half of it in a single swallow, barely tasting the notes of cranberry past all the vodka. Then she settled her back against the bar to look out over the crowd of beautifully dressed people. Where the hell were Quinn and Lucas? And what the hell was wrong with her, anyway? She was talking about her best friends here, not some strangers. She didn't have a goddamned thing to worry about.

"You look good enough to eat." His growl was low and intense in her ear and Ev had to resist the urge to shudder.

"I was wondering when you'd show," she said, feeling flirtatious and a little tipsy, more so when Quinn slid his kiss from her ear down the nape of her neck.

"You're getting her all hot and bothered, Quinny," Lucas said from her other side, surprising her out of the lust-filled haze, but only slightly. Ev didn't need to look over to see the expression on Quinn's face, because she knew it from all the other times Lucas had tried to get away with calling him *Quinny*. A horrible name, really. But this time, Quinn didn't even move his lips, just continued pressing those decadent kisses to her burning skin.

Then, thankfully, because she wasn't sure how much freaking more she could handle while just standing there at the bar, Quinn pulled back.

"I don't care where this dress came from, but I'm going to buy you twelve," he murmured, his voice husky.

The dress did look damn good. She was a little taller and a little bustier than Maddy Hollis, and Ev's breasts strained at the cups of the bodice, peeking out from behind a smattering of lace. Her curves were on full display in the flattering cut of the dress, and she wore more makeup than she'd worn to work all week. In short, she felt nearly as sexy in the dress as she did when she was naked in bed and Quinn looked at her with that hungry expression in his eyes.

"Tit for tat—let me see you," she said, pulling him from where he stood at her side so she could look at him properly. And damn, Quinn Langston looked good in a suit. She saw him in a suit nearly every damn day, but this was a Special Occasion suit and the crisp, tailored lines of fine Italian fabric made him appear even more untamed with a barely contained ferocity below.

"Keep that look to yourself," Quinn said, his eyes growing dark. "Or you're not going to be here long enough to get your rounds in."

She loved the promise in his voice, ached for it, for the knowledge that he needed her as much as she needed him. And she did need him. It scared her to admit, but it was the truth. Quinn was a part of her and Ev couldn't give him up if the world demanded it.

"You know, I could be filming all this to sell to an amateur porn site. At least that would make all the flirting entertaining for me." Lucas' dry tone was belied by the laugh that escaped.

"You flirt with anything that has two legs," Ev said, turning to face him.

She should have prepared herself, she really should have. At least seeing Quinn in a suit every day had helped her build up some immunity to the achingly sexy sight of him. But Lucas worked the streets with his unit, and his uniform was a pair of jeans and the faded black jacket he was never without.

But now. Wow, he cleaned up well.

But you already knew that, didn't you? You already knew how the sight of Lucas Vallejo in anything was capable of driving you to your knees.

And without permission, Ev's mind raced with images of her dropping to her knees right then, right there in this busy room, with her friends and colleagues all around her, of taking him into her mouth and...

"Something you like?" Lucas asked.

She should have been immune to that grin. Lord only knew how often she'd seen it turned on all manner of women, and quite successfully, too. But this time, when Lucas smiled, the expression smug and a little dangerous, Ev's stomach dropped and a warm glow swept through her, immediately followed by a haze of guilt. What the *hell* kind of game was she playing here, allowing herself to indulge in any of the untoward fantasies that would undoubtedly ruin her best friendships for life? Talking with Maddy and Lily about their unconventional relationships had clearly addled her brain, because the analytical, rational, intellectual part of her would have never even considered something so scandalous, something with so much potential to hurt the people she cared about most.

Of course, that didn't change the fact that when Lucas sidled up next to her at the bar and ordered himself a drink, Ev caught a whiff of his scent, of the rich leather of the jacket he usually wore, of the rawness and humor that mixed together to make the man beside her.

Quinn, Lucas and herself, they were all so different, cut from different cloths and fallen from different trees, but it worked, it balanced out in a way she would never have expected, and now, for the second time since befriending them back in training, she wondered if the scales might be tipping. The one instance of feeling out of her element with these two men had been when Quinn confessed to having romantic feelings for her and she had realized how quickly and truthfully she could return them.

But, God, *yes*, she wanted Lucas. As long as the thoughts were her little secret, the hidden fantasies of a woman who loved her partner deeply and loyally. In truth, she wanted both men. *Together.* At the same time, like Maddy and Lily had explained, like the natural, normal way it also seemed in her mind. *Together.*

A zing of desire shot right through her at the thought and Ev straightened, trying to pull herself together — a Herculean task, considering she was currently standing between two of the sexiest men she'd ever seen and they both smelled so fucking good. *Bastards.*

"You're all right," she said, scoffing and turning to look out at the crowd and hoping the pinching pressure in her thoughts didn't show on her face.

Except Lucas bent his head lower, nearly to the same spot on her neck Quinn had been kissing only a moment ago, and whispered low and full of promise, "Lying doesn't become you, Evvie."

The warmth of his breath across her neck made her want to squirm, but Ev was stronger than that. Besides, Lucas flirted with everyone. She'd had front row seats to it for years. Allowing herself to fall prey to his playboy traps was foolish and avoidable. And yet, it was so, so tempting to give in to this heady desire, whatever that meant.

"There's a caribou head over there that might enjoy your flirting," she said, eliciting a rough laugh from Quinn on her other side. God, how had she forgotten that he was still standing beside her? His large, powerful presence was usually the only thing in the forefront of her mind, but now she was torn, riding some imagined lusty haze that could only get her into trouble and nothing else.

"Come on, baby, let's dance," Quinn said, pulling her onto the floor before Ev could protest, before she could wonder if maybe he'd been watching the interaction between her and Lucas, wonder why he hadn't stopped it, but had rather, simply watched.

Because there's nothing there. Nothing is going on between you. Right. Of course.

Quinn led her through the bump and grind of their friends and coworkers on the makeshift dance floor of the Triple Diamond mess hall. A powerful beat pounded from the speakers, making the floor shake and sending the lights pulsing in time in bright flashes of pink and blue and purple. Quinn slid his hand around her waist and pulled her close, evidence of his obvious arousal pressing against her thigh and reigniting all the heat building from deep within her. Ev wasn't usually a sex-crazed maniac, but maybe there was something in the water in Wolf Creek, Montana, because she wanted to jump Quinn Langston's bones right in the middle of the dance floor.

Damn, the man could dance. He spun her around on the floor, moving in time to the ceaseless beat now resonating through her bones and in the push and pull of their bodies against one another. She'd never get tired of wanting Quinn, of touching him, of the way his body made her feel.

"You're so beautiful, Evvie," he murmured. The pet name from him was rare, but Quinn made it sound like the sweetest thing she'd ever heard and she ached from the way his mouth wrapped around her name. "I just want you to know how much I love you." The words cut through her heart and turned Ev into a glowing puddle. She couldn't help it. She had known from the start that Quinn struggled to express any deep emotions, but when he did, it made the whole world around them simply fall away and she ached at the sweetness in his voice, at the way everything he couldn't say by day melded to those simple words in the hollow of her ear. God, she loved this man, down to the depths of her soul. She belonged to him, just as he belonged to her.

"I love you too, Quinn," she whispered, her voice inaudible over the sound of the music, but Quinn smiled at her, the real, full smile he so rarely shared and she knew he had heard her.

"Do you trust me?" he asked, pressing his mouth to her ear to be heard over the roar of the music. Did she trust him? This man held her heart in his hands. Trust didn't begin to cover it.

Ev nodded and his grin got bigger. *Wolfish.*

"Just remember that, okay?" he asked.

Something twisted in her gut at his words. *Remember what? That she trusted him?* Why on earth would she need to remember that? It wasn't like there were some sort of test of their love and commitment to each other, unless he was about to tell her something she didn't know. But he had been acting a little more affectionately, more showy than usual since he'd found her at the bar.

She didn't get the chance to think further on it, because a pair of rough, calloused hands brushed her fingertips and, without turning around, Ev was suddenly and completely aware of Lucas by her side, moving to the steady thrum of the music and making it difficult to think. She looked over at Quinn, trying to gauge his expression to get a read on whether things felt weird to anyone else or just to her, but Lucas bent down and whispered into her ear before she was able.

"Dance with me, Evs?" he asked, the heat of his words making her skin tingle and ache in places that had no right to tingle or ache. But when he slid his hands from her fingertips to the crook of her waist, those places only ached more, running from hot to burning with the simplest of touches.

Panic shot through her and she glanced to find Quinn watching them, his expression neutral, patient, observing.

"Do you want to dance with him, Evvie?" he asked.

How the hell can I answer a question like that?

"Don't think, just tell me. Do you want to dance? With Lucas?" Of course, Quinn was a counterterrorism and negotiation expert, so the smooth, calm tone of his voice was as much an indicator of the oddity of this situation as a shaky, unsure one would have been on anyone else. "You said you trusted me," he continued. "So I'm going to need you to trust me now, baby. 'Cause if you want to dance with Lucas, I want you to dance with Lucas."

And I do want to dance with Lucas.

He must have seen the shift in her expression, because something glowed in those green eyes, normally so reserved, that made her ache. Then he began to move away, giving her the option he clearly knew she would never take for herself. But Ev was faster and grabbed him around the wrist.

"Both," she whispered, the word catching on the wild music or perhaps just the wildness of the beating in her own heart. "I want to dance with both of you. Together."

Red alert. Red fucking alert.

It's only a friendly dance. There's nothing to be freaking out over.

But, of course, dancing with Lucas now, when his body had been calling to her for months, when her relationship with Quinn made everything so incredibly off limits, was nothing like the friendly dances they'd shared in the past, at office parties or the bar after work. This felt different, somehow, weighted, loaded in a way she couldn't begin to understand, or rather was working quite hard not to let herself.

But then Quinn fit himself against her back, sliding all those familiar, delicious muscles against her, making it fucking impossible to think about anything but his hot, masculine body. *Bodies,* because then Lucas was there, his dark hair curling dangerously around his face, his eyes so intense and potent when he slid one finger down her cheek then the slope of her neck, the simple, seductive motion sending zinging need to her swollen nipples and throbbing pussy.

For once, since all this madness had begun, she didn't even care what was going on — she was too focused on the scents and sensations of having the two men touching her at the same time, of the sense of protection and comfort and rightness she felt when pressed between her two best friends in the world. *Friends.*

Because if she let herself get any further than friends with Lucas, she was looking at a whole world of trouble.

And yet, when he stroked her arm with those same promising caresses, she was tempted to throw it all out of the window just to reach up and fit herself to those swollen lips in what she knew would be a riot of passion they would never be able to box back up.

The song changed, and Lucas and Quinn both kept to the beat of the quicker music, riding and grinding against her. She wrapped her arms around Lucas' neck and held on tight. Quinn gripped her hips and Lucas buried his hands in her hair. God, the man's hands were intense—big and strong and rough from work. It almost made her wonder how they might feel on her bare, sensitive skin, the parts of her quivering for more of his forbidden touch.

"Just relax, Evs," he whispered into her ear. "It's only me."

Just Lucas, nothing to worry about. No need to stand on ceremony with Lucas. He's just Lucas.

Except then *just Lucas* pressed the softest, gentlest kiss to her neck and his touch sent a whole new wave of heat and need ricocheting through her. God, in that moment she couldn't have denied her desire for him if her life had depended upon it. Her nipples pebbled to tight points and her pussy clenched at the simplest brush of his fingers against her arm, sliding up her thigh, gripping her waist. It was rough and subtle all at once, a crazed ride that kept her mind tangled while she moved, Quinn at her back and Lucas her front, his eyes full of danger and intent she couldn't begin to read.

If she was smart, if she had any idea of which way was up right now, she'd put an end to this right there and then. But now that she'd tasted the apple, Ev wanted so much more. She wrapped one hand back, to cup Quinn's waist and pull him closer to her, and wound the other around Lucas' firm ass, taut below his dark slacks. The intensity and desire emanating from both men were so similar but so different at the same time. Quinn was rich bourbon, sliding down her throat, making her ache and pulse with spice and wild desire and anticipation. Lucas was a shot of whiskey, potent, promising, holding nothing back. He held nothing back now. The three of them ground to the music and Ev's mind turned to mush with each touch, each stroke of a hand across her neck, tangling in her fingers. Her mind ran rampant and her pulse buzzed with electricity ready to burst free.

Then the song changed. It was no longer the grinding, pounding beat of EDM, but a romantic, slow song that made her soul ache and the room quiet around them. Her senses jangled back into order and she opened her eyes against the onslaught of sensation caused by being sandwiched between Quinn and Lucas.

Oh shit. Oh shit.

Here she was in a room with her coworkers, professional colleagues and friends, and she was dancing on not one but two men who made her body ache with need and anticipation and Ev's heart nearly pulsed from her chest for a different reason this time. Complete and utter panic. Because the slow song, a song meant to be shared with a single lover, brought all this into stark, dangerous focus. What she wanted, what she knew she shouldn't want—it just wasn't done. Sure, Maddy and Lily Hollis had their men and it seemed to work for them, but no way could it possibly work for her, and if she had any sense at all, she'd stop before things got out of hand.

It might already be too late for that. Because she looked into Lucas' eyes, those deep, beautiful eyes, and found herself staring at a man with lust blazing through his veins, the kind of lust that both excited and scared her all at once, lust that made her burn for a carnal coupling they might not survive.

She stepped back, away from the temptation of Lucas' touch, and bumped right into Quinn, who steadied her waist.

"What's going through that pretty little head of yours, Miss Analyst?" he asked her. "Because I have no doubt you're overthinking something."

Overthinking, ya think? Maybe it has to do with this little game you guys think you're playing.

Nope. She wasn't going to indulge, wasn't going to give in. Instead, she did the one thing she could think to do, to get her head on straight and clear her mind of all the madness descending around her. She bolted.

Chapter Eight

The guest cabin wasn't far, but Ev hadn't thought to grab her coat before busting for the back door of the mess-hall-turned-dance-hall, and by the time she reached the cabin, she was freezing her ass off. Even the parts of her that had been so hot and bothered a second ago seemed to have cooled off with her brisk jaunt back, or perhaps simply the distance she now kept from the men who were both so capable of making her lose her mind.

Yes. I want Lucas. So fucking what? Except now that she admitted it to herself, as she dropped down before the fireplace to fill the grate and start a warm fire in the hold, Ev knew that admitting her misplaced desires for her best friend, the one who was decidedly *not* her boyfriend, was important. It was big. It was dangerous. Having sordid, secret dreams about him was one thing, but pressing herself against him on the dance floor... Against both of them...

Despite herself, Ev's pussy quivered a little and she had to resist the urge to run to the shower to take care of the messy desire business once and for all. Surely there was a reasonable explanation for Lucas' behavior, Quinn's too, with the things he had asked of her, to *just trust me,* and once she found out exactly what that explanation was, they could all go back to the normal way of things.

Yeah. Right.

"Now this is quite a sight for sore eyes." Quinn's voice felt like melted chocolate against her skin, like bourbon spilling over outstretched, inviting fingers. Even if she hadn't been in the process of building a fire, she would have warmed all over at the sound of him, no matter how angry and confused she felt in the moment.

"She does make a pretty picture on her knees, doesn't she?"

Ev resisted the urge to moan. Barely. Instead, she tightened her hand around the brick of the fireplace and willed herself to get a goddamned hold of the situation, of herself, before she did something she would undoubtedly regret. Of course, this couldn't be entirely classified as her fault, but she had to be strong here, had to hold off the impending carnal feast of indulgence she desperately ached for. She pushed up from the fireplace, but Quinn's voice stopped her.

"You're not going to deny Lucas such a pretty view, are you?" he asked. "I bet you didn't know we could see your panties, Evvie. They're soaked through, just like your pretty little pussy underneath. Is that from dancing with us?"

Quinn Langston was a man of few words, but when he got them right, damn, it was enough to make a grown woman beg, and here she was, already on her knees. But she ignored Quinn's words and stood, smoothing out Maddy's dress and trying to ignore her soaked panties sticking to her thigh. *Jesus, yes,* it was from dancing with them, from the ache their simultaneous touch brought on, the one she craved against all better judgment.

She took her time looking up, but finally couldn't delay any longer and lifted her head to look at them.

For fuck's sake.

Quinn had his arms folded and his back against the wall, legs crossed at the ankle. He almost seemed at ease, almost appeared *normal*, as if anything about this crazy night was normal, but the look in his deep green eyes promised her things, pushed her to the limits and back, made her want to taste the forbidden fruit.

He was leaning against the jamb, one arm high above his head, dark hair curling around his shoulders, making her want to reach out and pull her toward him, to muss up the hair and the dangerous, wicked smile on his face that she knew would make her beg for more.

Instead, she stepped back, putting space between her and temptation.

"What's going on?" Ev asked, careful to keep the husky tone from her voice, but she still wobbled a little, which both men clearly noticed, if the flash in Quinn's eyes and the tug of Lucas' smug lips were anything to go by.

"You're the genius," Lucas said shrugging. "What do you think is going on?"

"Flattery will get you nowhere," she said, her voice still a little shaky. What the hell was wrong with her, to be acting like this? What the hell was wrong with them tonight, anyway? And yet, Lucas wanted her to tell them what was going on, and there was only one obvious answer that came to her mind, only one thing that came from fitting all the puzzle pieces together.

"And distractions will get you punished." He winked, the same damn wink that had brought a thousand women to their knees in the years Ev had known him, the wink she had always thought she was immune to. Until... Until she had started dating Quinn. Until she realized that her ache for Lucas was there during the day too, that it haunted her during her waking hours, no matter how she ignored it.

"Now, we'll ask again, Evvie, what do you think is going on?"

Ev straightened. If she was about to go into battle, she sure as hell wasn't going to do it while questioning herself and everything the night could offer. The truth was, this would be an opportunity she'd never get again, and walking away from it might be something she regretted for the rest of her life.

"You're trying to seduce me," she said. "Both of you." She glanced over at Quinn and found his expression open, readable. He wanted this for her as much as she'd been wanting it for months. Of course, he couldn't possibly know the extent to which she'd been aching for Lucas' touch—she hadn't even admitted that to herself until right this moment—but he was saying yes, without any words, telling her that if this was what she wanted, then he wanted it for her too. *Well, damn, that's a heady thought.*

"Is it working?" Lucas asked. "Because, you know, we men have small"—he paused, his smile so dangerous she wondered if she might simply catch fire—"egos. We like to know when we're on the right track."

Quinn huffed out a laugh and Ev had to keep from choking on one of her own. Laughter wasn't really in her thoughts right then, though. Instead, all she could focus on was fight or flight. Or rather, if she'd stayed, it wasn't going to be the fighting kind of physical interaction.

"What are the rules?" she asked, instead of answering his question. She'd spent more than enough time living with both of them and dating Quinn to know that neither of them had anything to worry about in the *ego* department.

"There's our favorite analyst," Quinn said. "Let's just say you're our new case-by-case weekend, baby. You looked like you needed some cheering up, and Lucas so valiantly stepped up to the challenge."

"You're doing this to cheer me up?" She was incredulous and the room was beginning to feel quite warm. Perhaps she hadn't needed to make the fire after all. Perhaps she could have just stood around the two of them for a few minutes.

"Entirely a selfless act, I assure you," Lucas said, making no attempt to hide the grin on his face. "I won't even pretend to enjoy myself."

She very much doubted that was possible.

"So what, we just give it a go for a night and hope nothing gets weird?" she asked. "I don't want anything to get weird."

At that, Lucas pressed off the wall and stalked toward her. His movements were needy and powerful and he crossed the room in three long strides, grabbed her by the waist and pulled her flush against his body in one rough motion.

"We are not just going to *give it a go,* Evs," he said, lowering his head to her neck and growling the words into her ear.

Trapped against him like this, her daze returned and Ev found it difficult to think of much of anything at all, save the hardness pressing against her through two layers of fabric.

"If you accept this, *me,* for tonight, then we're going to make love to you until you lose your mind. We're going to torture you with pleasure until the image of you coming is ingrained in my memory for life. Together, we'll taste, suck and devour every inch of your quivering, succulent skin, then, when you're boneless in our arms, we'll do it all over again."

He licked the shell of her ear and Ev couldn't keep the moan from spilling across her lips, couldn't keep from arching into him at the divine, sinful thoughts thrust forth by his promising words.

"But you have to tell us exactly what you want," he continued. He ran his tongue down the nape of her neck, making it fucking impossible to think against the onslaught of pleasure and temptation. "Because we don't want there to be any regrets or misunderstandings, Evvie. We want you to have the best fucking night of your life without holding back."

She felt a little drugged at his words and when she lifted her head to look up into Lucas' eyes, Quinn crossed the room to join them. Before she was able to voice the question on her tongue, he beat her to it.

"It was my idea, Evs. If this is what you want, then I want it for you."

Then there was nothing holding her back, not the guilt of hurting Quinn, when he stood there giving her all the permission she needed, not the fear something might go wrong, nothing to keep her from reaching up and pushing a dark strand of Lucas' hair from his face before burying her hands in his dark locks and pulling him to her mouth in a blistering kiss.

Oh, God.

Lucas kissed like Dionysus, no control, no restraint. He drank from her body with the rampant joy of a Brazilian carnival parade, and Ev gave over to every touch, his indulgence in her mouth, the spanning of her waist with his broad, seeking hands. She lost herself to the taste of him, to the unleashed need that would send them both combusting before too long.

But finally, somehow, she pulled back. Her eyes were heavy with lust and when she turned to face Quinn, she saw something similar in his deep green gaze.

"Come here," she murmured, pulling him against her back and twisting to capture his mouth with her own. It was nearly the same position they had been in on the dance floor back in the mess hall, Ev captured between these two men, the hard caress of their bodies against her own driving her into a tailspin of desire. But it was different, too, because this time she knew the score and she refused to be a passive participant in the one night of her life where she could indulge in those secret, dangerous desires that might ruin everything. But there was no time for negativity or fears or early regrets. No, now she was going to make love to these two men just as they'd promised to make love to her.

"I guess I do have a voyeuristic streak after all," Lucas said, his voice husky against her neck. "What else are you going to do to him, Evvie?"

What aren't I going to do to him? To both of them? She broke away from Quinn to nip at Lucas' neck, while she started on Quinn's belt. They were still just standing there in the small living room, all their clothes safely on, and already Ev was losing her fucking mind to the heady sensation of being looked at like she was some rich dessert they both wanted to eat.

"Turn around, baby," Quinn said. She'd never understood the BDSM lifestyle, though lord only knew she'd run into it enough times in her job. But when Quinn Langston used that tone of voice in a command that she knew was about to bring her into a whole world of pleasure, Ev most definitely got it, and kind of, sort of wanted more.

"Or what?" she asked, but before the word was even out, Quinn's hands were up her dress, pushing it up her thigh. He wrapped his fingers around one of her plump ass cheeks and squeezed, *hard*.

"Don't be a brat, Evs," he growled. "Turn around and lean over the back of the couch." He squeezed harder and the sensation, the line between too much pressure and not enough, made her a little wobbly on her feet when she finally turned around and bent over the couch.

"More, Evs," Quinn demanded. "Show Lucas what a good girl you are."

Pleasure overrode her senses and Ev leaned down across the couch, her forearms resting on the pillows, her legs parted for balance. Just a few more inches and her dark purple lace panties would be on full display to both of them. The thought made a ripple of desire shudder through her whole body.

Then, before she could ask them to touch her, to do *something* that might help alleviate the pressure building deep within her, strong hands pushed her dress all the way up and spread her legs wider. She nearly stumbled, but Lucas, it was definitely Lucas, steadied her with a hand on her ass.

"So pretty," he murmured. "Do you mind if I taste, Evvie?"

Mind? Do I fucking mind?

"God, please..." It was the only thing she could get out. Spread wide and anticipating like this, all rational thought had fled.

"Not God," Lucas said against the small of her back. "Just us."

Then his mouth was there, pressing against her silk-clad pussy, making her arch against him with not nearly enough leverage. He tapped her ass and the sensation zinged through her, making her cunt pulse around emptiness.

But before she could demand, beg, ask him to please, *goddammit*, give her what she needed, his mouth was on her fully, savagely demanding her pleasure. The erotic slide of his tongue across the silk of her panties nearly made Ev scream and she clutched at the pillow, at the sofa, her pleasure mounting higher and higher, spiraling out of control.

"That's right, baby. Come all over his mouth." Quinn's voice was low and demanding and Ev's breath caught in her chest. Her mind whirled, her heart leaped. Then Lucas, his tongue still assaulting her senses, found the swollen nub of her clit and pinched.

She came undone, the world spiraling out from under her feet. She screamed Lucas' name and the pleasure captured her by surprise. She nearly lost her balance, but Lucas' strong hands held her steady when her knees began to shake and her shudders of after-pleasure coursed through her.

"Jesus Christ, Evvie. You're so fucking beautiful when you come." He slid back, caressing her wet pussy one more time before he stood.

"She is, isn't she?" Quinn's voice had the low, gravelly quality of a man already desperate, but holding himself back. "Want to test your voyeur theory, Lucas?" he asked.

"You asking if I want to watch you fuck her against the back of the couch?"

How could such crude words, words spoken like she wasn't even in the room, turn Ev's blood to molten desire? She was a proud, powerful woman in her own right, and yet the idea of Lucas watching Quinn fill her from behind, made her swollen breasts ache and her cunt pulse in need.

"Do you want that, baby?" Quinn stroked her back before palming her ass in his large hand. "Do you want to be on display for us? Tell Lucas and me what you want."

Like the bastards don't fucking know.

"Somebody fucking *touch* me..." *God, is that really my voice?*

"So needy..." Quinn moved his hand lower before he pressed the silk of her panties to the side and slipped one large finger deep into her waiting cunt. Ev jerked at the sensation, but Quinn steadied her hips with his other hand.

"Tell me, baby... What do you need?"

Ev tried to buck again, but Quinn's grip was firm. Instead, she growled, "Fuck me against the couch while Lucas watches... God, *please*."

Quinn moved back, pulling his finger free of her body, before the telltale sounds of his undressing carried through the small cabin. Then his hands were

Most Wanted

on her waist, sliding those soaked panties down her hips. Gently, he lifted one foot, then the other so she could step free of them. Ev spread her legs wide for him without conscious volition.

She thought he might make her beg again, but it seemed as if Quinn was already at his edge too, when he pressed the swollen head of his cock against her hole. She was so fucking wet he nearly slipped right in, but he held himself steady, waiting for something...

"Slow, Quinn. I wanna see you fuck her real slow."

A shudder of pure fucking lust beat a path from her brain to her cunt and Ev actually shook, just as Quinn pushed his large cock inside her. He paused with just enough of himself buried in her body to make Ev lose her fucking mind, then he carefully, slowly, pushed deeper, giving her what she needed at a pace so slow Ev wasn't certain she was going to survive.

"How's it feel, Evvie?" Lucas came around to look her in the eyes. He lifted her chin roughly and the power in the movement made her pleasure burn molten. "Quinn's got a nice big cock, doesn't he? How does it feel inside you?"

"Fucking big," she managed. "God, I feel stretched and...so fucking good..."

Quinn settled himself all the way inside her at that exact moment and she let out a whimper of insane need.

"I wonder how you'll take having two cocks buried deep inside you," Lucas murmured, his gaze so intense it might actually make her come right then and there. "I bet you'd love that, Evvie, being stuffed and filled to the brim."

There wasn't anything else she could do except nod, not when Quinn kept up his torturously slow assault on her body and Lucas whispered those filthy things to her.

"Have you ever taken a cock in your ass, sweetheart?" Lucas murmured, still caressing her face, her cheeks, her heated neck.

"Once." She choked out the word. "I... One time..."

He nodded, seemingly in approval. "Good. Then it'll be easier to fill you up later, when you ride both our cocks at the same time."

"I want you now..." Her voice was nearly ripped from her throat when Quinn hit a particularly sensitive spot deep inside her. "God, Lucas, please..."

Though his smile was smug, she could see the threads of his self-control wavering and she pushed on. "Fuck my mouth, please? I..." God, it was hard to think. "I get wet sucking cock..."

Quinn slid home just when she said it. "She does," he growled, his desire pulsing thick and full inside her. "You should hear the sounds she makes."

Lucas pulled his jacket off and laid it over the chair, then undid his cuffs and kicked off his shoes. He left his shirt unbuttoned, hanging open, baring a hint of the shadows and light caressing the powerful muscles below. He shucked his pants and came to stand before her on the couch in just a pair of fitted boxer briefs.

"Fucking tease," she growled, when he pulled back too far for her to lick the impressive bulge outlined against the cotton.

"Goodness, your mouth does need to be filled," Lucas muttered. "But I like to delay my gratification, so I'll listen to you beg for my swollen, leaking cock before I decide if you deserve it."

Jesus Christ, she'd only just admitted to herself that maybe getting ordered around in the bedroom wasn't the worst thing in the world and here she found herself in bed with not one but two Doms? Fucking great. *Fucking* great.

"You're pouting, baby," Lucas said. He looked like a hungry animal, standing there half-undressed, his body coiled in tight, complete control. "Quinn's right. You are a brat."

"I'm not pouting," she managed to get out, but it lost a lot of its luster when Quinn brushed his hand under her pussy and rubbed her slick, swollen clit. "Oh, *fuck.*"

"Now you've got the idea," Quinn murmured in her ear, his weight pressing against her back, sliding his thick cock deeper into her body at an angle sure to drive her to complete and utter fucking madness.

"Lucas, I... Can I please suck your cock?"

This seemed to please him and a predatory grin spread across his face, one that left no doubt in Ev's mind he planned to eat her up. Again. One hot FBI agent was a lot to handle, but two she might not survive.

Lucas stalked over to the couch and slowly, torturously slowly, pushed his briefs down, allowing his leaking cock to spring free into his hand. Ev's mouth watered and she bucked back into Quinn's thrusts. Lucas continued to tease her, sliding his hand up and down his thickness in slow movements.

Finally, blessedly, he stopped his teasing and moved close enough to brush his cock along the seam of her lips. The movement was somehow carnal and gentle all at the same time, and Ev's pussy pulsed hard around Quinn's cock. She opened her mouth and *thank God*, Lucas didn't tease her anymore, didn't make her wait to beg, just edged his cock between her lips and deep into her mouth.

He was bigger than he looked. His cock bumped the back of her throat and Ev schooled her breathing to take him deep, as he wrapped his hands in her hair and tilted his head back, eyes closed, like some ancient Greek god in the throes of wanton pleasure. The knowledge that she was the one causing such pleasure made Ev weak at the knees and she was grateful for the two powerful men keeping her steady and oh so happy between them.

"So good..." His words came out a jumble. "*Cariña*, I'm not gonna last if you do that." She sucked him harder, inhaling the masculine scent of sweat and leather that was so familiar and erotic all at once, so totally Lucas. She wanted to give him pleasure, especially as her own rose higher and higher with the pound of Quinn's cock deep inside her and the knowledge that she was stuffed between the two sexiest men she'd ever known.

Quinn changed his angle and hit her hard, deep, making bright lights flash behind her slammed eyelids and allowing her to relax enough to suck Lucas down even farther. He swore in Spanish, a tangle of street slang coming out in base, undulating need, and buried his hands deeper into her hair.

"Quinn, whatever the fuck you just did, do it again." His voice was guttural, rough and nearly broken. Ev could relate.

Then she couldn't do anything at all because Quinn drove deep into her again, hitting that spot hard, each new thrust a wave pushing her too close to the edge. The knowledge that her pleasure would be overwhelming and all-encompassing was both terrifying and tempting all at the same time.

"Evvie, baby, I wanna feel you come on my cock." Quinn sounded ragged and needy and she nearly lost her grip on the couch each time he pounded into her. "Please, baby, I'm begging you to come all over me."

He really was. The powerful, controlled, expert agent Quinn Langston was absolutely begging her to come on his cock. And the thought brought her so close to the edge that the next time he brushed her clit with his large, strong fingers, Ev fucking shattered.

She lost herself to the pleasure, suspended above her body for a breath, a frozen half-second before it all crashed down on her at once in a dizzying, overwhelming fireshow of pulsing need. She clutched at the couch, moaning around Lucas' cock and shuddering hard, wave after wave of sweet desire bursting through her.

Finally, slowly, her body came back into itself and she released Lucas' cock from her mouth long enough to get a breath in.

Quinn slid his hand up and down her back in a smooth caress and Lucas stroked her cheek, his eyes soft, full of a muted, gentle desire that was altogether more terrifying than the wild man he normally was.

"Can you come again for us, baby?" he asked, sliding his thumb along her swollen lower lip. Ev sucked it into her mouth without even thinking and he groaned, deep, thrumming through her. She shook her head and released his digit.

"It's too much," she managed, her voice still coming out in gasps, slow and achingly husky. "I...can't."

"I think you can," Quinn whispered. "We'll take care of you, baby. You trust us, right?"

Trust them? Hell, they're literally holding me up right now, since I can't possibly stand on my own two feet.

Still, she nodded. She trusted them with everything she was and more.

Lucas slid his cock across her lips to replace his wandering fingers, and Ev accepted it greedily, making him moan when she sucked him so hard and deep that he gripped the couch and let out a string of curses she couldn't possibly understand. Behind her, Quinn stroked her swollen clit, his fingers teasing between her folds as he oh so slowly slid in and out of her still-quivering pussy.

"That's right, Evs, nice and slow," he murmured.

And it was nice and slow and gentle and sweet and now that her head was back on her body, Ev suddenly didn't want nice and slow or gentle and sweet. No, now she was back to that stoking, rioting fire burning a path from one gorgeous man's connection to her body to the other and she was losing her fucking mind. With Lucas' cock buried in her mouth, she couldn't say so, however, so instead she arched back hard against Quinn and took Lucas deeper than before.

"Oh, fuck."

He didn't hold back. The only time she ever saw him do so was when he scoped the city streets, biding his time, waiting for the opportune moment. But Lucas Vallejo didn't hold back when it came to the passion she sensed coursing through him, the feelings now beating against her mind and body like the shores of an island during a hurricane. When he swore and when Quinn gripped her hips like that, riding her harder, tighter, higher, Ev lost the ground beneath her feet, lost the world around her and simply rode and rode and rode.

Lucas finished first. He pumped into her mouth once, twice, one more time, muttering in a bastard child of

Spanish and English and sailor about how *sweet her fucking mouth was wrapped around his cock.* His words stoked the last defiant tendrils of need within her and she burst free from her body in a swirl of pleasure that brought Quinn right with her, and he exploded across her bare ass until the three of them slumped against the couch, their labored breathing and the crackle in the fireplace the only sounds to break through the otherwise still cabin.

Finally, slowly, Ev came back into herself. The room was warm, though she wasn't sure whether it was from the heat of the near fireplace or the two large bodies beside her. Still, her skin goose-pebbled and she moved in an effort to right the dress on her body and maybe grab a sweater or six to keep her from ever touching either of them again. Because touching Lucas — touching Lucas and Quinn at the same time — it hadn't made her want him any less. Not even a little bit.

When you play with fire…

"She's thinking," Lucas said, pushing himself up from the couch and looking down at her. Quinn stood, too, grabbed a handful of tissues and wiped her skin clean with a gentle touch. Then he helped Ev to her feet, smoothing down her dress as though he didn't even realize he was doing it.

"Of course I'm thinking," Ev bit back, taking comfort in the knowledge that at least this bickering, intimate element of their relationship hadn't been completely warped by the madness in which they had just indulged.

Nope. The intimacy *levels here are just fine.*

Quinn ran his hands down her back, stroking her messy hair, which made a soft whimper escape her lips. It should have been sweet. It should have been gentle and comforting. They should have brushed their teeth in the mirror then climbed into bed together to read or watch a movie in domestic bliss. That was what the last few months of dating Quinn had been like, when they had been able to snag a few moments of said domestic bliss amidst the chaos of their jobs.

But right now, when she looked over at the dangerous, promising expression in Lucas' eyes, at the way his dark hair curled around his broad shoulders and his stance indicated no compunction with his half-naked form, Ev knew they weren't going to bed. They were *going to bed*, whether it was a good idea or not.

"The point here was for you not to think," Quinn murmured against her ear. It was so familiar and yet, it felt different too, like she had just discovered a new side of this man, a previously caged, controlled piece of him let free of its moorings. "But we know that's not really an option, so we can help. If you want."

He was giving her an out, a chance to acknowledge that this thing between them, it was a terrible idea. It could only lead to heartache and more trouble than it was worth. But though Ev considered herself a strong woman, capable of withstanding the tests and challenges life had long thrown at her, she wasn't strong enough to walk away from this.

"I want," she managed, shaky, nervous, excited. "I most definitely want."

Chapter Nine

Quinn didn't let her take another step. Instead, he picked her up and carried her into the bedroom, where he placed her down on the bed, Lucas close at their heels. The shade covering the enormous picture window was drawn back and showed that snow had started in the time since they'd last been outside, and that the world was a deep silvery-blue winter wonderland.

"Are you gonna close that?" Ev asked, without much conviction. She knew what their answer would be before they gave it, and she also knew, deep down, that she didn't want the curtain drawn any more than they did.

"Evvie, *cariña,* tonight is about your desires." Lucas was leaning up against the wall looking like sin incarnate, his Adam's apple slick with sweat and thrumming with every word. "Now tell us, do you want the curtain closed? Or do you want the risk of the whole world seeing what we're going to do to you tonight?

She shook her head, her voice somewhere else, her tongue all tied up.

"We want you to say it, baby," Quinn's voice was demanding. "Can you do that for us?"

Yup, definitely dealing with two Doms right now. Fine. She'd been handling their bossy, controlling attitudes for years, so she could more than handle them now.

"You two are very demanding." She jutted her chin in the air and tried for her best ice queen impression, the one that had helped her climb the ranks in the Bureau, even as a young woman. Still, with her hair mussed and her panties...somewhere...and the burning heat now building inside her again, the look probably missed the mark.

"You don't like it?" Lucas' smirk could have created an international incident. The man was too fucking sexy for his own good and he damn well knew it. Quinn, on the other hand, had her number.

"What are you planning, Evs?" he asked, those green eyes discerning and so dangerous for it.

She shrugged and settled back against the plush pillows right in the center of the enormous bed. Thank goodness it was so big. They were going to need a lot of space for the evening ahead of them.

"Just that I don't really need you two, ya know?" She slid her hand up her thigh, bent her knees and spread her legs wide to expose her now bare pussy, still so slick with need and tension and her recent releases that Ev honestly couldn't tell if she was coming or going. Or coming and coming and coming. Before they could stop her, she slipped a finger between her folds and deep inside her body, hissing at the contact with her still sensitive flesh. She heard twin inhalations of breath and stroked deeper, bringing herself higher and higher on simply the thought that they were watching her toy with her clit and stroke her needy cunt.

"Go slower, baby…" Quinn sounded far too in control for Ev's liking, so she did the opposite of what he asked and pressed a second finger into her pussy, pounding her body faster and more erratically. Amazing. She was actually close to another orgasm even after all the pleasure they had just shared. She honestly might not survive the night.

"That's enough." Lucas was on the bed in a flash, holding her wrists still in mid-motion. Her cunt quivered and Ev let out a string of curses under her breath. He nipped at her neck, at her chest, at her collarbone as he held her in place. "The only thing I want to see in your tight little cunt is my cock, do you understand?"

Oh, she understood. She also understood that while the Dom thing *totally* turned her on, she enjoyed fighting with them way too much to just roll over at a few choice words.

"Or what?" She rocked against her hands, giving herself none of the release she so desperately needed.

"Or I'll put your over my knee and spank your pretty ass red until you're dripping all over my fingers, then I won't let you come. How does that sound?"

It sounded like maybe she might roll over at just a few choice words.

"Stand up." This time, Ev did as she was told, disentangling herself from her fingers and Lucas' grip, before coming to stand at the side of the bed. Quinn's gaze tracked her every move and she felt the heat like a physical caress. It should have been disconcerting, but the three of them had been dancing together for years. Communicating like this, in this new way, with their mouths and bodies, felt nearly as natural as sharing beer and pizza and arguing over what they were going to watch on TV.

"Strip, Evvie, slowly." Lucas' voice had an almost lazy quality to it, but she saw the way his jaw pulsed and the taut need in his eyes and she knew he wanted *more* almost as much as she did.

So she didn't argue. Instead, she slid her hands down her hips to reach the zipper at the top of one boot then the other, her ass high in the air. Then she kicked the boots off and slowly began to pull the dress down her body until her breasts plumped free, her stomach was bared and fabric pooled at her feet on the floor.

And in the moment, standing before them wearing nothing but her mingling pride and desire, this all felt real. This all felt like she wouldn't be able to go back. Lucas and Quinn were here, in front of her, looking at her with admiration and desire and affection so clear in their eyes, and Ev's heart felt a little fuller. Of course this was wonderful. This was them.

"God, you're so fucking beautiful." Lucas' words were harsh and guttural and a little surprised, like he hadn't meant to say them. And that felt too real, too much, so Ev smiled at him then pushed the unbuttoned shirt off his shoulders and onto the bed.

"You both have three seconds to get undressed and join me on the bed," she said with a grin. "Or I'll see if Maddy Hollis and her husbands are looking to experiment tonight."

That got Quinn off the wall in an instant, with what sounded like a growl.

"Like hell you will," he said, undressing slowly, his movements still controlled and powerful, despite the obvious thread of jealousy running across his voice. Wasn't that funny? He'd invited Lucas into their bed, but the idea of sharing her — *sharing her, wow* — with another man, even as a joke, turned him into something carnal. Of course, with Lucas, it made sense in a way it couldn't possibly with anyone else.

Then Quinn was standing beside her, gloriously naked, gleaming in the light of the few candles around the room and the soft light from the falling snow outside. But for once, it wasn't enough just to have him. This time, she needed Lucas too. She shot him a pointed look and unlike Quinn he practically scrambled to get his pants and shoes off, into a ball on the floor.

"So…" She laughed, her confidence faltering for just a second. "How does this…work? Should we play Twister and just start putting our hands places…or — "

"You're tense," Quinn said. "Lie down on the bed and let us take care of you, okay?"

She hesitated for only a moment before climbing back up on the bed and turning to lie down with her head facing the vista outside. They moved slowly then, and not knowing when or where they might touch her made Ev's body tremble with anticipation. Strong hands massaged the backs of her calves, slowly, patiently, working out the kinks she had sustained on the dance floor and right in their shared living room. Those were Lucas' hands. His were worker's hands, calloused and hardened. Quinn's had been once too, but he spent more time in an office now than he did on the streets of Kabul, and his hands had softened just a bit, no longer shaped to fire a gun or limber enough to cover his face from falling debris, though he still did both.

She knew Quinn's demons well, knew Lucas' too, just as they knew her deep fears of settling down, of becoming everything her parents had always wanted for her. It wasn't war or street violence, but Ev's inner need to be more than another Portuguese-American girl from Newark made her shoulders tense and her teeth grind. It was the knowledge that even if she did just that, exactly the way the storybooks told, she still couldn't keep her family safe, her friends safe, not really.

"You really have to learn to turn off that oversized brain of yours." Quinn's voice now, and he brought his hands to her shoulders, strong and expert. He beat back the knots that formed whenever Ev remembered why she refused to settle down, why her fears of becoming just another person who lived just another life were compounded with the knowledge that she could do everything in the world right and bad things would still happen to her.

"He's not here, Evvie. He doesn't need to be here." Quinn, expert at his job, expert at *her* that he was, always knew when she went back to *that* place, to that night over twenty-five years ago, when her world had been shattered.

Quinn had been nineteen when he'd left for his first tour of the Middle East. Lucas used to say he first realized East Los Angeles wasn't paradise when they found a bullet lodged in the frame of the bunk bed he shared with his younger brother and they started sharing the bottom bunk. He'd been eleven when that happened. Ev. Her stories. Her demons. She'd been eight.

Longest amount of time to get over it, then.

But, of course, who got over the expression on their best friend's face when she stood, shell-shocked, dark-red blood staining the faces of Tinker Bell and Peter Pan on her flannel pajamas? Who could get over their own?

Whoever got over the knowledge that someone had killed their next-door neighbors, while they hid, that this made the fourth family in the neighborhood and eighth in the state? Clearly not her, since she'd gone into a life fighting the kind of people who had robbed Carly of a childhood and Ev of any sense of normal.

"Evvie, look at me." Ev looked up, or rather, Quinn tilted her chin up with a gentle hand, demanding her attention. "Where are you right now?" She tried to shake her head free, but he held it strong. This wasn't the first time he'd walked her through these memories.

"I'm here."

Quinn shook his head. "You're not here, Ev. Do you want to be here?" Here, as in *now*, as in *Montana* as in *thirty-five* and not the terrified eight-year-old watching through the slit in the bathroom closet as the serial killer later known as Peter Buldark hacked Carly's parents and older brothers to pieces in the hall.

"Of course I want to be here, Quinn," she managed. "Sometimes it just comes back." *It*, the memories of those nights, of the lineup she had held Carly's hand to go look at, despite her mother's protestations, of the trials. It hadn't come back in months, even years. Why the hell was it returning when she should have been focused on the best fucking night of her life?

She sat up, suddenly feeling a chill that had nothing at all to do with the snowstorm outside or the bareness of her skin. Lucas was still beside her on the bed, and he pulled her into his lap without another word. She let him, let herself rest her head on his shoulders, let herself be sad, let herself give in to the sensations of Quinn's fingers running up and down her skin, as she remembered.

For just a moment.

But these men, her best friends, they made the memories fade a little, like dust plumes in sun streaks, and after a few deep, steadying breaths, Ev came back into herself, a sudden weight off her shoulders she hadn't realized she had been carrying around.

"Better, baby?" Lucas asked. He knew the stories of her childhood just as Quinn did. Between the three of them, there weren't any secrets. Except for the one where she'd spent months wanting to sleep with both of them and now that she had the opportunity, she was rehashing old serial killer cases.

The first serial killer case. For me, at least.

But if she wanted to psychoanalyze, and lord only knew she was good at that, there'd be plenty of opportunities for it later. This whole getting fucked six ways to Sunday thing was a once-in-a-lifetime opportunity.

"I'm okay now," she said. PTSD, of course. In her line of work, she'd always assumed PTSD where killers were concerned capped at a certain threshold. Apparently, it took a sense of calm and comfort to make her feel the most vulnerable.

"You're always okay," Quinn said. "You're the strongest woman I know." He yanked his briefs up his legs and Ev frowned.

"Flattery isn't going to distract me from the fact that you're putting your clothes back on..." she said, raising one eyebrow. It often happened like that, the memories — sometimes flashbacks, sometimes just memories. She'd come out of the darkness so relieved to see that she'd be giddy for it—which was probably inappropriate, but she'd long since stopped caring about the different ways she coped.

Quinn only shook his head and disappeared into the other room. She could hear him in the kitchen and that comforted her for the moment, so she turned to look at Lucas instead. God, she was still in his arms, muscled, powerful arms, banded with tattoos—an homage to Los Angeles, tangles of thorns around names, each one a niece or nephew, a clock because he never knew how long he had, a cross.

She traced the cross with her fingers. It was simple, blocky and black and ran across the sinew of his upper arm.

"When was the last time you went to church?" she asked, with no idea where the question had come from. Lucas raised a brow.

"Probably ten years ago," he said. "For one of the kids, I'm sure."

She tilted her head up to look at him and, even now, with the tension her memories had stirred, Lucas was still one of the most beautiful men she had ever seen. He played at the hard-ass just like she did, but his eyes were stained glass of deep browns and golds and his hair was soft under her fingers, almost as soft as the skin of his chest. For scientific purposes, she ran her hand down his abdomen, enjoying the way his muscles tensed under her touch.

"Evvie," he said, his voice almost a question. Good, it was satisfying to know she could make this man lose his steady grip on the world around him. "What are you doing?" She pulled back, but he grasped her wrist and held her there. "I didn't say to stop. I just asked what you're doing."

"I like touching you," she said. The words sounded strange because they didn't sound strange, because she did like touching him and because for the first time since the dangerous desire had overtaken her, Ev was allowed to do just that. The problem was that she feared her own liking it far too much.

Problems are for the morning. This is now and it's the only damn chance I'll get.

"You can touch him, Evs." She turned to see Quinn leaning against the doorframe. He was a big man and he took up the air in the room by just standing there, dark muscles and dangerous smile. A bottle of dark whiskey dangled from his fingers. "That's why he's here, for you to touch him."

Lucas' cock twitched against her leg and that familiar glow invaded her senses all over again, riding up her spine and making her feel heady and dizzy at the thought. Nothing was going to interrupt them now. No way. She was going to enjoy them to the freaking fullest.

"Can I have that?" she asked Quinn, indicating with her chin. His smile was so wicked her pussy wept hot and needy. Fuck, she'd just come about fifteen times in a row and if she didn't get one or both of them inside her in the next five minutes she might spontaneously combust.

"The whiskey?" he asked. "Or?" His cock bulged, hot and heavy behind those navy briefs, and Ev's mouth actually fucking watered.

"Both, now," she said. "Drop the briefs and come here."

Quinn must have been as surprised as she was by the commanding tone, because he actually did what she asked him to and set the whiskey on the bedside table, then he dropped his drawers and joined them on the sprawling bed.

"Lie down," she commanded him. *Commanded. Ooh, this is nice. I like commanding sexy alpha men to do my bidding.*

She climbed off Lucas' lap to grab the bottle of whiskey, and he moved with her, positioning her body so she was resting on her hands and knees. He then began a slow assault of kisses against her inner thigh. Ev opened the whiskey and splashed some across Quinn's bare chest. She took a moment to simply enjoy the view, the way the gold liquid contrasted with his dark skin, how his abs constricted when she stroked a hand down his centerline. Then she leaned down and licked, capturing the spicy drink on her tongue as it mingled with Quinn, all Quinn, stark, controlled masculinity, the softness he rarely shared, the love deeply cared for. Quinn Langston was a man of many emotions and he had opened himself to her to share them all.

She put the warmth of her love for him into every lick and suck and taste of his contracting muscles, of his peaked nipples, straining under her touch, of the curses spilling from those kiss-swollen lips.

Behind her, Lucas teased in the same slow and demanding way. He ran his mouth up and down her thighs, never touching her where she most needed to be touched, never giving her the pressure she so desperately ached for. Until finally, finally, he pushed her legs apart, forcing her to spread her pussy wide to him, still slick and glistening with her last release and the building need to reach her pleasure again.

"So fucking pretty," he murmured, his gaze hot, while Quinn watched her with those knowing eyes, his control threadbare and hazed over with lust. "I could eat your pussy every morning, Evvie, and it wouldn't be enough for me." He swooped down and kissed her swiftly, far too swiftly for the contact she really needed. "So sweet." He plunged a finger deep inside her. "And so fucking tight. I can't wait to see the way you take my cock, baby."

Ev tried to ignore him, she really did. Instead, she traced more whiskey kisses up and down Quinn's hard, muscled chest, pausing to nip his neck, which made his cock twitch against her belly. She wanted that cock, wanted to feel both of them inside her.

'Have you ever taken a cock in your ass, sweetheart?'

God, just the once and, though it hadn't been horrible, she hadn't been able to see what the big deal was. But now, with Quinn below her and Lucas above her, she really, really wanted to find out.

"Lucas." His name came out a groan, torn from the depths of her throat. She had tasted him before, teased him with her tongue and mouth and desperate kisses, but she wanted to feel him inside her, wanted to know the way his cock stretched and filled her pussy, and she didn't want to wait for it.

Lucas slid another finger deep inside her body and Ev bucked forward, brushing against Quinn's erection, which poked her in the belly. A slow, lazy smile spread across his face and she leaned down to kiss his smug expression away, but the kiss turned on her when Quinn threaded his hand through her mussed hair and slid her down for a blistering kiss that had them both moaning. Lucas took the opportunity to lift her hips higher and plunge another finger deep inside her.

Ev was a mess. Her brain was shorting out and all she could focus upon was the heat of Quinn below and the way Lucas filled her with his fingers. Her body was running needy and desperate and no one was touching her enough to put out the kindling fire burning oh so hot within.

Behind her, Lucas bent down and kissed her ass cheek. He dug his teeth in and she yelped at little at the sensation, before he slid his fingers out.

"I'm going to get a condom," he murmured against her skin. She would never get tired of the feeling of him touching her skin, running his mouth and fingers against her.

She looked up at Quinn. His green eyes were on fire, sparking dangerous explosions that made her heart ache with love and admiration. He knew what she was asking and her heart felt a little freer when he gave her the nod signifying just how much they were on the same page.

"I have the implant," she managed, her voice husky and rough. "And we're... I'm... It's all safe..." Wherever her brain was right now, it had taken a vacation from this room with its overwhelming erotic heat. *Probably for the best.*

"You're sure?" Lucas said, brushing her back as he settled down on the bed again. "I have protection in my bag. I always use it, of course, and my last department check came back clean, but you don't have to, Ev."

When she turned, he had shifted his gaze back to Quinn. It should have bothered her, but it didn't. Each step they took tonight—and after—they were taking together, and complete communication was the only way this could ever work.

"I'm sure," Ev said, catching his gaze. "We both are."

This was just about sex, so why did her chest feel so heavy at those words? Why did her brain decide now would be a mighty fine time to make a comeback?

Poor choice of words.

"Now, less talking." She tried to sound bossy, but damn, she just wanted him too much for that. She slid her hand down to the connection between her body and Quinn's and slowly began stroking his engorged cock while Lucas settled his weight behind her. She loved the feeling of Quinn's cock in her hand, of the smooth, swollen weight of him, the way he jumped and throbbed at her touch.

Then she couldn't think about anything but the visceral sensation itself because Lucas was lining his throbbing head up against her hole.

"Such a *fucking* tease." The words were ripped from behind clenched teeth as he rubbed her slightly, far too slightly. "Lucas, I swear to *fuck.*"

"What, baby?" he asked, leaning over her. His weight was warm and erotic against her back and pressed her further into Quinn's hardness. All three of them groaned in unison. "What are you gonna do to me if I don't fuck you, huh? You know I like to hear you beg, maybe that'll do the trick."

Her breasts were swollen, her clit glowing hot and needy, her cunt already wet and spilling down her quivering thighs. Ev wasn't above begging.

"Stuff me with your cock, sir," she gasped. "Please."

Sir. Oh damn.

By the way Quinn's cock pulsed against her belly and Lucas' strained to slide into her hole, they had both experienced the same shooting eroticism that followed the use of the word.

"Making it really hard for me to resist you, *cariña.*"

"Then don't fucking resist." She barely managed to get the words out of her mouth before Lucas shoved his cock deep into her cunt.

Ev came. The sensation of being filled, of her swollen cunt pressed against Quinn's throbbing cock, of literally being pressed between these two men, made her lose her fucking mind and she screamed while wave after wave of insane pleasure beat through her. Her fingers clenched around the blanket, but it was only because of the two pairs of strong hands around her waist and ass that she didn't collapse.

"Fucking love it when you scream," Quinn's voice in her ear now. "Love watching your face while you lose control. You're the goddamned most beautiful woman in the world, Evvie."

She surged against him, the motion sending fireworks of desire through her still-quivering clit and pushing Lucas deeper into her. They held her steady, and she finally found a rhythm stroking Quinn's cock with her hand as Lucas slid deep and slow in and out of her throbbing pussy. They murmured filthy, erotic words to her, and she tried to keep up, but the pleasure was overwhelming and intense and almost too much.

Then she felt Lucas at her ass. His finger was slick and she didn't have the brainpower to wonder if he'd brought lube or if it was just her own arousal. She tensed, but he stroked in and out of her body slowly, making her relax, making her give in to the invasion of his finger against the tightness of her hole. He pushed his knuckle in, then another, until he was buried deep inside her and her senses shut down, tuned in to nothing but the fullness of his cock in her pussy and his finger in her ass and Quinn's erection pulsing against her swollen clit.

"You have to relax, baby," Lucas murmured. "We want to take you like this, right here, but you're gonna have to relax."

She was strung so tight she thought she might pop into a dizzying explosion of lust and pleasure and he wanted her to *relax*.

Apparently, there was some communication going on above her head, because Lucas slowly pulled out of her pussy. She clenched on the space where he had been, desperate for that filling, stretching sensation, but undoubtedly more relaxed to his exploring finger. He slid another finger into her asshole to join the first and Ev almost lost her balance right then, but one of Quinn's strong arms came around her waist and held her steady, his other hand slowly, gently massaging her clit until the dual sensations were pushing her to places she'd never been before.

"Can you take another, baby?" Quinn asked, low and taut. She wasn't sure how, but she nodded and Lucas slid another finger into her, this one definitely slick with lube and her chest got tight with the breath she was holding as the pleasure threatened to overwhelm her every sense.

"I'm going to slide inside you now, okay?" Quinn continued. "You tell me if it's too much." It was already way, way too much, but the best kind of too much and Ev shifted enough for him to brush her sensitive hole. He pushed in only a little, just so the head of his cock rested against her opening, then Ev was surprised to find it was her moving, her pushing down on his hardness inch by inch until she was seated completely on top of him, his hard cock buried so deep in her pussy, Lucas' wandering fingers still exploring her tight ass.

But despite being too much, it wasn't nearly enough and she turned her head to look Lucas in the eye. He was almost as wrecked as she was, his control long since shattered and the look of a wild, unleashed animal all too apparent in his deep brown eyes.

God, how on earth am I going to survive him?

He carefully, slid his fingers from her tight hole and lined his cock up with her entrance. He grabbed what had to be the small bottle of lube from before and drizzled a healthy amount over his cock and fingers, before brushing the entrance of her hole with the excess. A small bout of nerves erupted in her belly, but they were gone as soon as they had come. These were the men in her life she trusted more than anyone. They knew her darkest secrets, her most hidden fears. If she could trust anyone with her body, it was the two people she'd already trusted with her mind and, in many ways, her heart.

"I'm ready," she murmured. Lucas' smile was so sweet, so adoring that all Ev wanted in that moment was to make him as happy as he made her.

Slowly, so incredibly gently, he pushed into her ass.

No matter which way they sliced it, this was going to be a very tight fit. Ev's ass tensed around the invasion and Lucas slowed, allowing her to grow accustomed to him before trying to move again. Quinn ever so slowly moved his hips and Ev rested more of her weight against his chest to better take them both.

After slow, long moments, Lucas bottomed out inside her and they all three let out a collective breath. Her mind and body were overwhelmed with the insane pleasure of it all and Ev barely knew which way was up and which way was down for the erotic bliss descending upon her body, rocking through her core to the person she was deep inside.

These men did that to her, together.

They must have been communicating, because they both gently began to move at the same time, sliding oh so slowly from her body before pushing back in her. Even the gentle motion was so intense, so overwhelming, that each thrust pushed Ev higher and higher to the peak she'd been desperately seeking. This wasn't going to be an orgasm — this was going to be a fucking detonation.

A low moan escaped her lips when Quinn's pelvis brushed her clit at the same moment Lucas pushed back into her ass. The gentleness was sweet and loving and adoring and Ev appreciated them for it, but the low burn at Lucas' entry was gone and now she needed more than sweet and loving and adoring. She needed everything.

So she began a rough rock between the two men, taking and giving, wrapping herself around both cocks with a speed and desperation it only took them a moment to match. Then, oh God, oh *fucking God,* they were riding her in earnest now, giving her the full, adulterated drive that pushed every single thought from her head except how fucking hot and deliciously erotic it felt to have two huge cocks stuffed inside her.

She was so close, so fucking close to the pivotal point and her whole body screamed in desperate need of release.

Quinn reached for her breast in the same second Lucas slapped her ass and Ev lost herself right then and there. She screamed and jumped off the edge of pure, unmitigated lust.

Her orgasm must have set them off, because Quinn groaned hard then gave himself over to it, spurting hot release deep inside her cunt when he lost control to the pleasure. Lucas followed two thrusts later, pulling free to empty himself across her back, as Ev writhed under the onslaught of her bliss-filled waves.

Her eyes began to droop closed and Quinn shifted out from under her. Two sets of warm, strong hands caressed her skin clean with a soft towel, massaged her body to bonelessness then positioned her under the blankets on the soft-as-heaven bed. Distantly, she heard Quinn murmur to Lucas, *Stay. She'll want you here.* Then two warm, very naked men slipped into bed, one on each side, and Ev fell into sleep.

Chapter Ten

Quinn was out of bed and halfway across the room before he woke up. His five years in counterterrorism meant his phone could ring at any hour and he'd jam the buttons before opening his eyes.

"Langston." Shit, it was fucking freezing in this room. Even the padded carpet was cold against his feet. The fire in the living room had died in its hold hours ago, and now that he was no longer in Ev's warm arms, he felt a chill down his whole body.

"Oh good, I caught you." Lydia Brandenwell made Ev's ice queen impression look like a Disney movie. His boss was brash, rough and a woman who had been crossed far too many times in her life to let anyone else ever do it again. She was nearly seventy, if Quinn had to guess, and had spent more than half her life in the United States military before retiring to the much more subdued position of director of the FBI's counterterrorism fly teams.

"What's going on?" Quinn spied his briefs from under a pile of clothes and shoved the phone under his ear to yank them on. Speaking on the phone with his boss, one of the most powerful women in the country, while buck-ass naked wasn't a new phenomenon. After all, he'd been called into work from a dead sleep more times than he could count. But doing it while he was buck-ass naked after a raucous erotic night with his two best friends felt like a horse of a very, very different color.

"Cool your jets," Brandenwell said. "No national emergency to speak of at the moment. I just wanted to be in touch about those Cordell files. I know I gave you until you got back, but I'd like them today, if you could."

Quinn glanced over at the clock above the bed. It was early. Though it was difficult to gauge the time of morning with all the snow outside, he was still surprised to find it was only just past six. *Good, I have the time I need.*

"The Internet is a little spotty out here," he told his boss, yanking on a pair of jeans that might have been Lucas'. It was dark in the room, lit only by the light of new-fallen snow, and he was too tired to give much of a damn. "I'm going to head down to the main house and work on it there. It shouldn't take more than two hours."

Curth Cordell had been on their radar for months now, and a small cache of new information had come in that might or might not prove interesting.

"That's fine," Brandenwell replied. "I know how much Sam and Aimee mean to you and I don't want to pull you away from their wedding. But it's important this gets done today."

"It will."

She gave him a curt acknowledgment then they hung up without ceremony, plunging the room back into complete stillness. Quinn interrupted it only long enough to yank a sweater over his head and dig around for the wool socks he was damn happy he'd packed. They got winter lite in DC, but the snowstorm from the night before appeared to have coated everything in a thick layer of frost.

Of course, it was also possible he was stalling. He'd looked out of the window, at the floor—for his clothes, of course—at the clock on the wall, but he still hadn't brought himself to look down at the bed.

Because you know exactly what you're going to find there. You've known what you were going to find for months.

Quinn wouldn't call himself a coward. He'd spent nearly a decade in the Middle East and now worked for counterterrorism. He didn't scare easily. At least, not about most things.

But when he considered the idea of a life without Ev Monteiro by his side, his heart got tight and a thin sweat broke out across his neck. She'd been his everything from the day he had met her in training all those years ago, and when they'd first acknowledged their feelings for each other—by falling into bed together after a night at the Greek embassy—Quinn had only been able to conclude that he was the goddamned luckiest man on earth.

It turned out life was a lot more complicated than that. Or perhaps it was a lot simpler.

Finally, slowly, he turned to look at them. Ev was still facing the empty pillow where he'd been lying only a few minutes earlier, her body tucked tight—against the cold or his absence, he couldn't be sure. He loved to watch her sleep, the way her face relaxed when she was truly resting, the way she let her guard down, even if that did let her demons in every once in a while. They all had their own nightmares and that was part of the reason they'd all come together so seamlessly. Trials and tribulations could make for great bedfellows.

Quinn almost choked.

Bedfellows. Literally.

Lucas was wrapped around Ev's back. His head was resting on her shoulder and one arm had a possessive wrap around her. The blankets kept them covered — after all, it was freaking cold in the room — but Quinn knew they were both bare below, pressing heated flesh and skin to heated flesh and skin.

He watched them, their breathing in tandem, their bodies pressed so naturally together, watched them and waited.

And it didn't come. He'd been expecting…*something.* He'd been expecting jealousy, possessiveness, anger, *hurt.* But he didn't feel anything.

He didn't even feel surprised.

And that was the biggest kicker of all. Because as much as Quinn wanted to be shocked and awed by the oh so natural sight of his girlfriend and their best friend tangled up in the bed together, he couldn't be. Not really. In fact, it felt a lot like the rain clearing after a storm. He knew what was out on the road, but now it was bright and stark and impossible to ignore.

Hmm, that would give him something to think about for about as long as he could pretend he didn't know exactly why he wasn't surprised or any of those other raw emotions.

But instead of indulging in the thoughts, he walked over to Ev's side, padding slowly on the carpet. He sat down on the bed and reached out to stroke the strands of dark hair off her face until she stirred under his touch. An unhappy sound escaped her lips and she looked about three seconds away from jumping out of bed, but Quinn leaned down and whispered in her ear.

"Just me, baby," he murmured, still stroking her face, as if trying to assure himself she was really here. "I have to go work for a little bit, but I'll be back."

She didn't open her eyes, but she was gaining consciousness. "Where are you going?" Her voice was rough from a night spent voicing her pleasures and Quinn took no small amount of pride in that.

"Mess hall," he whispered. "But Lucas is here, you'll let him take care of you this morning."

She gave that sleepy grin that made her normally reserved face look so adorable Quinn's heart actually felt fit to burst. "Shirking your duties?" she asked. "That's not like you."

He rolled his eyes, though he knew she couldn't see, and kissed the top of her head, slow, lingering.

"I'll be back in a little bit to give you the good morning you deserve," he promised, his voice coming out more growly than he would have expected. *Hmm*, it turned out there was a little bit of jealousy hidden deep down there somewhere. A very little bit. "I'm just putting the option on the table."

He went to move away, but Ev caught his wrist, her eyes open only a little, sleep clinging to her. "I love you," she said.

"I love you, too," Quinn replied, brushing his mouth across her knuckles. He was pretty damn sure he was on his path to proving exactly how much.

Lucas was having one hell of a dream. He was more comfortable than he'd ever been in his damned life and pressing bare flesh into one sweet, soft ass, his body both hard as a tire-iron and relaxed, at ease, as if he was finally where he belonged in this big crazy world.

"Lucas." The sound of his name reverberated through his whole body and made him ache, made him want, made him press harder into the saccharine sweet pleasure consuming him. "Jesus, Lucas…"

He came awake slowly, taking in the unfamiliar room, the starkness of the white world outside and the least familiar thing of all. It wasn't exactly new for him to have a woman in his arms. It was new for him to have *this* woman in his arms, and for a moment all he could do was blink at her. And throb against her sweet, tight ass, because apparently his body hadn't gotten the memo that last night had turned into today and *oh, hey,* he'd left his glass slipper behind at the castle.

"You're being a tease." Her face was half-buried in the pillow, her voice muffled, but still he heard the husky, needy sound that sent an ache of desire straight to his balls. He could have her three times a day for the rest of their lives and it wouldn't be enough, and, of course, he wasn't allowed that.

"I should probably go." God, when he had he gotten so fucking good at controlling himself? Certainly not last night.

"Don't you dare." Even with her face full of pillow down, Ev could command a damn army. More heat. More need. If he didn't get out of this bed soon he was going to lose himself in her sweet cunt in all of about five minutes.

"I don't think it's a good idea," he managed, his voice actually cracking.

"Then don't think." Finally, she turned to face him. Her hair was mussed and spilling over smooth, bare shoulders. Her lips were swollen and so delectable it was all he could do not to reach out and taste her. But it was her eyes, the desperation and need and potent ache in them that very nearly broke Lucas' control. "Quinn…" She paused. "He had some work to do this morning, but he said the same rules apply." Now she was actually hesitant and Lucas could have just about kicked his own ass for that. "If you want them to."

Want them to? As if he wasn't harder than fucking steel from just sleeping at her side. *Want them to* — he nearly laughed but caught himself at the last minute. Instead, he moved closer to her, until his cock bumped against her belly and slid up the smooth plane of her abdomen.

"Does it feel like I don't want you, Evs?" he asked. "Do you think for a moment I don't want you?"

She sucked in a breath at the contact then shook her head. It was pretty remarkable, that. Ev was just about the strongest person he knew. She walked the walk and she took control of every situation. She had never been a woman to back down from a challenge and he knew exactly how hard she worked to keep her life and her job in neat, organized lines. Ones he'd just thoroughly tangled. But right now, when she looked so utterly disorganized, so full of heat and unleashed need that stoked such a fire within her, Lucas felt like he was on top of the goddamn world.

"What about you, Evvie?" he murmured, asking the question he already knew the answer to. "Do you want the same rules to apply as they did last night?"

She didn't reply, at least not in words. Instead, she found his hand and guided it from his hip to the apex of her thighs. Slowly, carefully, she pressed his index finger to the heat between her pussy lips.

"Does that feel like I don't want you?" she asked him, amusement tangling with the evident desire in her voice. "You make me ache, Lucas. God..." She laughed and the sound came out husky and desperate. "Please don't make me wait. Not this time."

He didn't respond. Instead he lifted her chin with his free hand until their eyes met. Desire mingled with humor and something more raw, something that looked a hell of a lot like anguish in those pretty golden-brown eyes. That, he couldn't fix, not now, not this like. But he could give her what she wanted. He stroked his thumb across her bottom lip before slipping it into her mouth. Ev pulled him back into her mouth instinctively and Lucas groaned at the sight and sound of her sucking his finger. She'd sucked his cock last night, in the throes of erotic haze, but this somehow felt more intimate, more intense than even the feeling of her wrapped around him there.

Of course it feels more intimate. You're alone.

Guilt seized him for an instant, but it relaxed in a haze of confusion and lust. Yes, Quinn was gone, not there to...to what, *chaperone? Give permission?* Nothing so trite as that. His absence and their continued contact certainly added to the growing intimacy, but that wasn't it.

It was morning. It was the next day and Ev still had her fingers wrapped in his hair, tangling and pulling when Lucas freed his digit from her mouth and began to move it down her chest to the hot, peaked point of her swollen nipple. He circled her rosy flesh before pinching the nub between two fingers and squeezing.

Ev arched, pressing his swollen cock more deeply against her inner thigh, and Lucas sucked in a rough breath.

"You like having your nipples touched?" he asked her. He wasn't usually this vocal in bed, but with Ev the need to demand and control and reassure drove him to the edge. *She* drove him to the edge.

"Yes…" She hissed out the word when Lucas pinched her with more intensity then bent down to suck her into his mouth. Her breasts were full and so sweet and achingly swollen and he slipped his hand free from the heated apex of her thigh, enjoying her small whimper of disappointment when he did, to cup her other breast in his hand.

"Have you ever come from just having your breasts touched?" he asked, the words spilling free from his mouth before he'd had the chance to think about them. But Ev didn't appear to mind, not if the twisting of her lithe body below him was any indication. "I want you to come now, baby, just from my playing with your delicious breasts. Can you do that for me?"

When she caught his eye, her face was already wracked with pleasure and Lucas simply grinned and continued his sensual assault on her needy, desperate body, ignoring the near-painful throb of desire in his own. Instead, he set himself to the task of making her buck and arch and moan and grasp the blanket in needy, tangled motions.

"Lucas." She could scream his name until the day she died and it still wouldn't be enough to sate the fire deep within him. "Lucas, it's too much."

"It's not enough, baby," he replied. "Not nearly enough." He scraped his teeth along her breasts and she nearly shot up off the bed. He'd gotten the impression she enjoyed a little pain to go with her pleasure the night before, but he ached with the driving need to dominate her, to have her at his mercy as he was so clearly at hers.

But not now. Now was for the intimate. Now was actually a goodbye. And that meant *not ever*.

But even the maudlin thoughts couldn't distract him from Ev's climbing moans and he brought his hand up to stroke the side of her breast before administering a light slap. She inhaled sharply, carried by a soft curse, and heat flooded her pussy, spilling a little onto his leg. Damn if that wasn't about the hottest fucking thing that had ever happened to him in his entire life.

Then he pulled his hand off her breast and slapped the flesh harder, enough to make her grasp at the bed below her with a force from deep within. He did it again, his other hand still tracing and pinching and teasing her swollen nipple when he brought his palm down against her breast. She was bucking in earnest now and he pressed his mouth to hers in a kiss made of savage, carnal desire. They bit and sucked at each other's lips and tongues and he continued the slow assault on her breast—light, demanding taps increasing in speed until Ev broke off the kiss, arched her back and screamed into the morning air.

"*Fuck, Lucas, fuck. I'm…I'm coming…*" Her words descended into a tangled bramble of half-curses and moans and he relaxed his fingers on her and let her ride the wave of pleasure until she slowly returned, her body shaking and flushed and a fucking delectable sight.

"You, now." Her voice was demanding but wobbly and husky nonetheless, like she was holding on to everything she had. Lucas knew the feeling all too well.

He pressed up against her, their faces aligned as he put the head of his swollen cock to her wet pussy. God, she was so incredibly wet, and he knew she'd be hot and tight and capable of making him lose his ever-loving mind.

He kissed her, slow, long, putting all the things he was afraid to say, afraid to acknowledge into that one lingering kiss, and it released so much emotion it overwhelmed him. It overwhelmed Ev too, because when he looked in her eyes, Lucas was surprised to see a sheen of moisture, though he wasn't entirely sure if that was her or the filter of his own vision. So sweet and hot and tight and waiting for him. Ready for him. He'd been ready for her for so, so long. And now, in a cruel twist of fate, he only got enough of a taste to make him absolutely lost.

"Please, Lucas." Her words were so raw and needy, he actually complied with her demand, pressing himself into her inch by inch, kissing her while he did, slow and lingering and steady until he'd bottomed out inside her tight little pussy.

"Oh my God." She stared in wonder at him as her body stretched to accommodate his cock. "Feels so good, Lucas." She clutched at him like she couldn't quite find purchase in this carnal ride they were on. This sweet, soft kissing and low voices and desperation, was so much more dangerous than anything they had done last night. It had the power to break him.

Ev had the power to break him.

"Can I move?" he asked her, afraid to say a word more than necessary, lest he spill the secrets he'd been keeping even from himself these long months.

Ev nodded, her mouth pulled taut, her cheeks flushed, her lips swollen. "Please." Her voice was wrecked. He pulled out slowly until he was nearly free of her body and desperately, wantonly aching to be back inside her. Then he gave in to what they both needed and pressed back in, filling her, feeling the rush of heated tightness around his cock. She squeezed him, accepted him and demanded of him and he gave her all she needed and more.

They rode each other then, clinging tight to backs and shoulders and arms as the heat and demand and need and far-too-close intimacy began to settle like a warm blanket over them. Lucas committed Ev to memory, the feel of her taking him whole, the brush of her soft, swollen breasts against his chest, the taste of her lips on his mouth, the desperation in her eyes that he couldn't help but feel went deeper than the physical burn between them.

Then there was nothing but that burn and the way her body and his fit tight together, the way she felt wrapping him and how his balls pulled tight and his cock swelled with every new plunge into her body.

"Evvie, I need you with me." The words pulled taut from the back of his throat. "God, please, baby."

She clung to him, though he doubted she knew how hard, and now around swollen, bitten lips. "I'm with you, Lucas. I'm with you."

She shattered on the last, squeezing so tight around his body, coming hard, so fucking hard her pussy seized and swallowed him in rioting pulses, which sent Lucas into a tailspin of aching, bursting pleasure. He lost the world around him, lost the bed and the cabin and the mountains until it was only him and Ev and the chaos of pleasure between them. He burst hard, pulling himself free of her body just before he exploded, painting her belly in his release, sending him into a deep spiral of carnal, possessive lust that wracked him through the aftermath of pleasure.

It took a few moments, but they eventually came back to life, the small cabin filled with the steadying sounds of breathing, and Lucas couldn't stop himself from pulling Ev close and holding her to his chest. He'd never be able to do this again, and that settled things in his mind.

I need to walk away from this.

A maudlin thought for the glow racing up his spine, and he tucked her head into his shoulder so she wouldn't see the heat behind his eyes or the betraying flush of his cheeks. He could have her to himself for just a few minutes longer and he'd be damned to hell if he wasted it.

They didn't speak. Not when Lucas pulled a few tissues from the bedside table and gently, carefully wiped her body clean. Not when he pulled her back into an intimate embrace that kept them closer than they had been all night. With sleepy eyes, Lucas glanced at the clock on the far side of the bed. It was still early. They had time—not much, but they had time. All the rest of it could wait for a little while. With Ev's head resting against his shoulder, their arms and legs tangled together, Lucas finally closed his eyes and allowed himself to sleep.

Chapter Eleven

Ev woke in a frenzy. The room was unfamiliar and the bed was unfamiliar and the body she was pressed up against was most decidedly not her boyfriend's, though it was hard and delicious beneath her fingers and she jolted to full alertness to try to figure out what the hell…

What the hell actually summed it up pretty nicely.

It only took a moment for her to get her bearings. Of course, it was Lucas lying next to her, pressing his hard, muscled body into her back, stirring desire inside her even though she knew their time was over, that it *had* to be over, or she would risk far too much. This had been nothing more than one night of erotic, uninhibited fun and now everything was going to go back to normal.

Jesus, how the fuck can things go back to normal?

Because she'd had Lucas. She'd had Lucas last night and she'd had him this morning and the lust she had been running from for months, the one she had finally indulged in, was no weaker than it had been before. In fact, even one look at his sleepy face, at the brush of kohl-dark eyelashes against his soft cheeks, at the muscled chest bared to the room, and Ev's desire ran rampant, stronger, more powerful than ever before. She had wanted him, she had had him, and now she knew exactly what he was capable of doing to her.

What they were both capable of doing to her.

Fuck. People don't do this. This is...

Except people totally *did* do this. Apparently. Since Maddy and Lily Hollis were both happy as fucking clams with their lovers, their *husbands*, big masculine men that she would have taken one look at and assumed they wouldn't be caught within ten feet of another man's cock, but who had apparently all been more than happy to jump into bed with one woman.

Fuck, I don't know. She was overwhelmed and frustrated and not really sure which way was up. Goddamn, she studied the vastest reaches of the human psyche for work—albeit, mostly the ones that turned a person into a serial killer—but through her undergraduate and graduate programs and subsequent training with the BAU, she'd been exposed to nearly every walk of life on God's green earth.

So why the fuck was it so hard to believe that she might actually want...

What? A relationship with both of them? Yeah right.

"I come in peace, Evs." Quinn's voice cut through her circular and none-too-helpful self-flagellation of the morning.

She looked up. Quinn wore a dark green and cream sweater over a pair of nicely fitted jeans. The green complemented the lightness of his dark skin and the emerald shade of his amused eyes, and he looked about good enough to eat, especially when he gave her his rare smile. Even in a cozy sweater, Quinn was still all power and control and raw masculinity.

This is nuts. How can I still want more? After all I had last night?

But, God help her, she absolutely did want more.

"What?" It took a moment for the words he'd spoken to settle in and she cocked her head to the side. The motion caused the sheet that had been draped over her chest to slip free, baring her breasts to the cool room. Quinn's gaze darkened, but the smile never left his face.

"You've got a murderous expression on," he said. "I just said that I come in peace." He handed over a travel cup of coffee just when Lucas started to stir beside her. Ev tried not to fidget, but her expression must have given away some of the obvious discomfort she felt, because instead of his normal *I'll talk when I'm dead* attitude about most of the things in his life that bothered him, Quinn sat down on the edge of the bed and looked at her with so much empathy and affection in his green eyes that Ev's head nearly exploded.

This *thing* between them, all of them, it was far more complicated than it would have ever been if Quinn had simply grabbed a stranger off the street for their erotic night of pleasure. Of course, she would never have gone through with it if he had grabbed a stranger off the street.

It's only Lucas. It's only ever going to be Lucas that fits in, just…fits in.

"Brought you coffee," Quinn said to Lucas, who sat up looking far cuter than he had any right to. His rich skin glowed in the soft light from the winter wonderland outside, proof it was still fairly early, and his dark hair curled around his shoulders, looking mussed and adorable and like she'd been yanking it all night long in the throes of passion.

The truth was a bitch.

"I'm going for a walk," Ev said, trying to keep her voice to an even keel and missing it by a country mile. She cracked on the last word, practically sloshing coffee on Lucas when she handed him the cup Quinn had just given to her. She was out of bed so quickly the cold floor barely registered below her feet and the brush of fresh winter freeze made her skin actually feel good — her burning, hot, confused skin. As for the rest of her, the weather wasn't going to do shit where that was concerned, not if the temperature jumped to ninety and Wolf Creek, Montana, suddenly got a heat warning.

"Ev." God, had he ever sounded like more of a negotiator in the whole time she had known him? Right then his voice made it seem like she was a breath away from setting off a bomb and he was the only thing keeping her from doing so, not like she was about to walk out of the room, the room where...

Where what? Where she had all the potential of setting off a figurative bomb in the most important relationships of her life.

"Don't..." She pulled a sweater over her head, grateful for the added protection. And it was definitely Quinn's. Nice. Wonderful. At least she knew she wouldn't accidentally grab either of their pants, given the significant size difference in asses.

What does it matter, you've already been in both their pants. Bad time for puns. Very bad time for them.

She found her jeans on top of her duffel bag and yanked them on, then the wool socks, then she headed for the living room.

Quinn was behind her first. By the time Lucas came out of the other room, he was wearing his flannel pajama bottoms – or maybe those were Quinn's, too. What the fuck ever, they'd shared each other's clothes in the past. Hell, she'd been stealing both their clothes pretty much since day one. But the idea of wearing them now – it felt all kinds of topsy-turvy.

"What's the problem, Evvie?" Quinn asked. Lucas was leaning against the doorframe behind Quinn, his arms crossed and his pose almost relaxed, except that Ev knew better. She knew so, so much better, and the clicking tension in his jaw and the way his face pulled taut were all indications he was absolutely on edge.

And the fact that she knew it, not only did she know it but she wanted to put him at ease any way she knew how, that right there was the problem.

Sleeping with them hadn't been the problem. It had been amazing and incredible and showed her a whole new world of pleasure and desire that even now Ev ached for. But sleeping with them had *shown* her the problem, and if she acknowledged what had gone on between them, how it had fundamentally changed something inside her, she would without a doubt ruin the two most important relationships in her life.

"What's the problem?" Her voice cracked. *Fuck.* She'd faced down goddamned serial killers and hadn't so much as batted an eye, but right now, with the formidable force of the two men before her, making her want despite everything else, Ev was losing control. And that pissed her off. "This… We should never have. Fuck. What if this makes things weird, huh? Was it worth it?"

Makes things weird was like calling a high alert code *something to be concerned about*. This wouldn't make things weird — it would *destroy* them. All of them. Her relationship with Quinn, her relationship with Lucas, the guys' relationship with each other. And the idea that they wouldn't be what they had been for the last five years to each other — that scared Ev more than just about anything she had seen in her job.

"It won't be weird," Lucas said quietly, hanging back in an uncharacteristic move of restraint and defiance. To whom? Who's in charge here? It sure as shit wasn't her. "Ev, if you can just tell us what the problem is…"

"This." She motioned to the room. "We fucked it all up. *I* fucked it all up, by letting this happen. I should never have let any of this happen. Not last night. Not this morning." She glanced at Quinn when she said it, because *hey*, if she was going with self-flagellation she might as well hit the gas. The corner of his jaw ticked almost imperceptibly, but Ev saw it nonetheless. Yeah, this wasn't good. None of this was good, despite how very good it had felt last night.

"It may not feel weird now," she said. "But it's different between us now. You can't deny that it is, and I hate that. I hate the idea that we're not as strong as we were."

Quinn took a step toward her, but Ev pulled away and grabbed her coat off the back of the couch.

"It was just sex," Quinn said. "We made love, nothing more."

She scoffed. "Made love. No, babe. We fucked, all night long we fucked, and it felt great. But now it doesn't feel so great, does it?"

It didn't feel great to say those words, not when they weren't true, not when Ev knew in the back of her mind that no matter how rough and crude and intense their sex had been, it *had* been making love. At least for her.

They didn't understand where she was coming from. That was clear on both of their faces. Maybe they had really both believed things could simply go back to normal once the sun rose. Maybe, if the circumstances were different, if *she* were different, they might have. But they also didn't know the secret she'd been running from for months, the one Quinn had mistakenly believed to be a bad mood caused by work or family stress, the one that didn't just threaten to ruin everything between them now, but already had, in a fundamental, cracking foundation sort of way.

But Ev couldn't say any of that. And right now, her throat tight with unshed tears, her face burning with fear and frustration and anger, she couldn't say anything at all. Instead, she yanked her coat on, turned on her heel and, for the first time in as long as she could remember, if she didn't count the night before, Ev played the part of the coward and fled.

Lucas watched her go in a tangle of winter clothes and hair and cold wind and he felt like a weight had settled right in the center of his chest. For a second, he couldn't breathe, couldn't get air back past the choked-up knot in his throat, and he knew that, despite the lack of articulation, despite the obvious emotion that had twisted Ev's words into something hurtful, something cruel, she was absolutely, undeniably right.

He felt like he was watching himself move over to sit on the couch. At some point, Quinn had started a fire in the grate, because the room was warm and cozy. Lucas didn't feel any of that comfort, though. His skin and his chest and his mind all felt frozen with the knowledge that, *yep*, he'd made a colossal fucking mistake.

"Did I miss something?" Quinn was the one leaning against the wall now. Lucas hated when he did that analysis thing, looking too close at a person's nonverbal tics to see what they were hiding, what you wanted, what you were willing to die for. Most of the time, that last one was reserved for the terrorists they encountered, but Lucas wasn't entirely certain it didn't apply here too. "This should have been fine, right?" He cocked his head to the side and stared at the door Ev had just run out of.

It is fine. It should be fine and it is fine and…

"What am I missing, Lucas?"

Fuck. If he'd known it was this fucking hard to have a secret living with two other FBI agents, he would have picked friends in the civilian sector.

"Maybe you should go after her," he said, instead of replying to Quinn, because what he really wanted to say, what he really wanted to tell him was on the tip of his tongue and if it came to light, there was no going back. Not in the *we slept together in a big old pile last night* way, but in a way he'd never be able to shut back up.

"She doesn't want me to," Quinn said. "She wanted to be alone to process this, whatever *this* is. I'll find her in a few minutes."

Then he came over and sat down next to Lucas on the couch, filling the space with his presence and making the weight and guilt and hurt in Lucas' chest feel both so much heavier and so much lighter. *That was what friends were for, wasn't it? Being there when you needed them even if you didn't want them? Crowding your personal space when you didn't know what was best for you?*

And Lucas had gone ahead and committed the cardinal sin of friendship. Or rather, he'd finally acknowledged that thing deep inside himself that meant there was no going back to the way things were.

Quinn placed his hand on Lucas' shoulder and Lucas smiled. They'd been through a hell of a lot together, each of them fighting their own demons, together. Each of them running to the Bureau, and away from the things they'd left behind, Ev's in her neighbor's closet nearly two and a half decades earlier, Quinn's on the streets of Kabul, Lucas' in East Hollywood. To speak nothing of their jobs and the horrors they faced each and every day they went into work. Another thing that tied them all together.

That past was just one more reason Quinn deserved the absolute truth and so Lucas finally lifted his head out of his hands and turned to look at the man he'd called brother for nearly five years.

"I'm transferring." There, that was easy.

Coward.

Quinn blinked, but didn't show any other signs of even having heard Lucas. So he barreled on, sure that once he started he wasn't going to stop until the whole sordid tale was out there for the world to see.

"The Los Angeles office has an opening and they want me. It's closer to my family and I...I can do some good in my homeland, ya know? Clear the streets I walked as a kid." He scrubbed his face with his hands and wondered why this was the hardest conversation he'd had in recent memory. "I wasn't sure, ya know? In fact, I've been going back and forth on it for a while. But I think I'm going to accept. I think... I think it's best."

Because I tasted the fucking forbidden fruit and it didn't make me want her any less, didn't make me...

"Why?" Quinn was remarkable at that, at not putting any emotions into his voice. It was the only way one worked in his field. But Lucas knew him better and he knew that Quinn was probably feeling both confused and hurt right now, and the last thing he wanted to do was make this harder for any of them, because lord only knew it was damn hard enough.

"I thought I could stay," he muttered. "When you and Ev first started dating. Hell." He laughed, the sound self-effacing and more bitter than he felt. Or thought he had felt. "I actually thought I was happy for you guys. Imagine that, right?"

He took a deep breath, because this wasn't going to be the first time he said it out loud. It wasn't going to be the first time he told another person. No, it was going to be the very first time he acknowledged it for what it was in the months since the feelings had first churned his gut and left his heart cold.

"I love her, Quinn."

He turned. Quinn's eyes were soft. Softer than Lucas had expected them to be, but then again, maybe this hadn't been the revelation for his best friend it had been for Lucas. The thought made his shoulders sag a little and a small amount of weight lift from his spine, the tension in his back loosening by a fraction and a half. Quinn—and Ev, of course—they'd forgiven him for a lot. No, things couldn't go back to the way they had been before all this, but they might be able to forgive him and that *mattered*.

"I thought I'd be able to touch her without losing my mind," Lucas admitted, and was it just him or was the sound that came from his throat a little tight and pinched and husky? "I was wrong. Being with her last night, this morning, it only made those feelings real. Strong. Dangerous." Not a flicker of surprise in the other man's gaze. That was good, at least.

He stood, because he was sitting there in his goddamn pajama bottoms, and Quinn was fully dressed and had been up and working while the moon was still high in the sky and wasn't that just the way of things between them?

Of course, he couldn't bring himself to hate Quinn. Not even now.

"I think moving is the best thing for all of us," he said. "Because you guys deserve a chance and…and so do I."

Then it was silent. The fire crackled in the grate and the wind brushed the windows and rustled the bare trees, but the silence was one between Lucas and Quinn, a silence where Lucas truly didn't know what Quinn was going to say next — or if he even deserved to hear it.

"I thought I'd be more surprised by this." In truth, Quinn didn't sound surprised at all. "But I also know what it's like to love her, so maybe I'm biased." He chuckled against his hand, brushing his mouth as if deep in thought. Lucas paced, his movements frenetic as a caged beast. Quinn sat there looking fucking dignified and handsome and in control of a situation there was no getting control over.

"I would never do anything to drive you two apart," Lucas said quietly. "But I also can't stay here. Not now. Not after what we've done together." And not with the knowledge that she would always be so incredibly close to him, and yet farther away than the whole distance from Los Angeles to DC.

"Of course not," Quinn replied. "I…I'm not quite sure what to say here." Quinn Langston, unsure — Lucas had seen everything. "I know we would miss you if you moved." He shook his head before Lucas could interrupt. "We would both miss you. A lot. And I also understand why transferring feels like the right thing to do." He paused. "Does she know? Is that why she left like that?"

Lucas shook his head, the familiar guilt settling heavy back in his stomach. "You're the only person I've ever said it to. Including myself. I think she's just afraid of ruining our friendship, but that one is all on me."

A humorless laugh, if he had ever heard one.

Quinn looked like he was about to say something, but a phone buzzed on the kitchen counter and he glanced away from Lucas then grimaced.

"Brandenwell is up my ass about this file," he said. "Hang on. Just... Just hang on."

Yeah right, like there was anywhere for him to go. The Triple Diamond Ranch might have spanned about three miles in every direction, but he couldn't run far enough or fast enough to clear his own head. Plus, with his fucking luck, he'd probably stumble upon some blissfully wed orgy involving one of the Hollis sisters. Was it technically an orgy with three people? It didn't matter—chances were he'd see Ev next, and that was one he really couldn't bear.

I don't want to leave her. I don't want to walk away. Not from either of them.

But he also didn't want to flay himself on the cross as he watched the two of them slip deeper into their powerful, long-term relationship, one that would eventually include a place of their own, one that would never include him the way he now understood he wanted to be included. Or something.

Fuck. Just *fuck*. That summed it up pretty nicely.

Quinn chatted quietly on the phone for a while, his face back to an impassive mask, and Lucas found a long-sleeved shirt on the back of the chair and tugged it over his head. No use in being naked during his nice little pity party. Eventually, Quinn signed off then slipped the phone into his pocket.

"She needs me to look at something." He was apologetic now. "It's urgent and can't wait, but this conversation isn't over. And I think, before you make any rash decisions, you need to speak with Ev. Okay? Don't accept the job yet."

It was the most he had said since Lucas' confession and Lucas nodded a little dumbly.

"Okay," he said. His voice was distant and didn't sound familiar to him. Quinn gave him a somewhat tight smile then headed out of the door, shutting it behind him. Just like Ev.

Lucas shook his head. If he had any goddamn sense, he would be the one to walk away next time, before anyone else got the chance to do it first.

Chapter Twelve

The barn was warm and comfortable, and Ev understood why she'd stumbled upon Lily and Micah in there the first night. It was sweetly erotic, with strong scents of hay and firewood and flannel, and it made her ache to be held, caressed, kissed.

But, of course, aching to be held, caressed and kissed was what had gotten her into this fool mess in the first place.

She should have fucking known she wouldn't be strong enough to keep her feelings separate from her desires. Deep down, she *had* known, of course. But she'd wanted him, wanted the whole thing, more than she'd cared. And this was her hangover to show for it. Fitting, since being with the both of them together was intoxicating and spicy and hot across her tongue and lips and neck...

A soft moan escaped her mouth and Ev couldn't have told herself for a million dollars if it was out of lust or sadness. Were they mutually exclusive? It seemed like they should have been, but her body still hadn't forgotten any of Lucas' touches or tastes or the way he'd felt inside her, and goddamn it, that was part of the problem.

"Ev, is that you?" Her shadow came into view first then Lily stuck her head around the stack of hay to where Ev was sitting.

Hiding. Like a coward.

"Hi, Lily." Her voice cracked. What would the folks who'd called her the ice queen have to say now?

"Don't *Hi, Lily* me," Lily said. She was a tall woman, willowy and thin, but her arms were muscled and when she set her shoulders and jaw, nothing about her would blow down in a stiff wind. "We shared clothes. We're way past informal." Ev didn't want to admit exactly what had happened in those borrowed clothes. Lily crouched so they were eye level, her dark brown gaze far too knowing for comfort, and Ev just rolled her eyes.

"Whatever you're going to say, just say it."

Lily opened her mouth, but before she got the chance to say anything, the door opened again and, a moment later, Maddy Hollis joined them in the warm, cozy corner of the barn. It was a good thing it was still early, otherwise she'd be showing up to this wedding smelling like horse.

"Oh dear." Maddy went full older sister in a second. Ev had two sisters of her own, confident, brash, outspoken women, who had busted on her and their brother through most of her childhood but would have both been first in line to defend her in a fight to the death. Maddy's expression was nothing short of ferocious, though it was clear she was trying to hold back.

"Which one hurt you, love?" she asked. She didn't bother to crouch, but simply settled against the wall a few feet from Ev, fire in her eyes. Sympathy and patience, too. "I bet it was the pretty one. It's always the pretty one because they're used to getting away with everything."

Ev raised an eyebrow, trying not to smile. "Which one is the pretty one?"

"Lucas, obviously," Maddy said, at the exact same moment Lily said, "Quinn, of course."

Both of Ev's eyebrows went up at that. "Scouting my men, are we?" Their expressions changed at the same instance Ev realized her slip. "Not my men. I mean, Quinn is my man, but Jesus, I was just kidding. Lucas is my friend, not my *man*." She was rambling and Maddy and Lily Hollis were letting her, because without a doubt they both knew exactly what was going on in her head.

So Ev decided not to beat around the bush. *Jesus, what fucking good would it do, huh?* Ev was smart. She was well-educated and street-smart and knew a hell of a lot about people, about what made them tick, about what made them do good things and bad things and the whole spectrum between. But when it came to a matter like this, she was on foreign turf. No use in denying a tour guide.

"I slept with them last night," she said quietly. "Both of them. Then Lucas again, this morning. Alone."

And why that felt like some sort of confession, Ev wasn't quite certain. Quinn had essentially given them a free pass to do whatever they wanted to do. It wasn't like she was cheating.

Not physically cheating, maybe, but that wasn't fucking. That was making love. And in order to make love...

Nope. No way, no how, nope, nope, nope. Except…

"So instead of talking about how your feelings for Lucas go deeper than you want to admit — confusing feelings, because, of course, you still love Quinn from the bottom of your heart — you ran away and hid in the barn so you don't have to face them."

Lily Hollis was damn smart for being such a little bit of a thing.

"Who said anything about love?" Ev asked. *Psh*, she had, with the infusion of misery in the question.

"You didn't need to say a damn thing," Maddy said. "We get it. We've both been there, remember? This isn't simple territory to navigate, maybe even more complicated for you than it was for either of us. But it's not impassable."

Ev shook her head. "I'm not having this conversation. I'm in love with Quinn. I'm going to go home to DC and everything is going to go back to normal."

Lily cocked her head, sending a cascade of hair swishing all around her.

"Is it?" The question didn't push. It was a simple, basic, common question. And Ev couldn't answer it honestly without facing up to some pretty raw truths. Because no, things weren't going to go back to normal, not when every time she saw Lucas fresh out of the shower, she would remember all he had done to her body, all that lay below his simple towel. Not when every time he had a woman over, she would be undoubtedly overtaken with a need to throttle the woman in his room, the one who wasn't her. Not when every time she made love with Quinn, she would be remembering that night and wondering if he knew how she felt, hoping he didn't because she'd never, ever want to hurt him.

"What do I do?"

She hadn't meant to ask the question, but it had come whispering out, soft and fragile, the very first admission she had ever spoken aloud of maybe, actually potentially...trying? Was that even the right word? God, she didn't know. She didn't know jack.

"It depends on what you want," Lily said cheerfully. "That's the question you have to answer first. What do you want, Ev?"

And that was the question Ev had been denying for five months, two weeks and a handful of days, since Quinn had first kissed her on the balcony at the Greek embassy or she had kissed him, and she had allowed herself to be happy, to be so, so happy, until two nights later, when the dreams had first started coming — dreams that looked a whole hell of a lot like exactly what they'd done last night. And this morning.

What do I want?

It was absolute madness to ever consider it, and yet... It was that *and yet* hanging over her, making Ev doubt. She didn't like to doubt. In fact, she wasn't very good at doubting herself. But this...this wasn't a one-decision kind of thing.

She looked down at her toes. She hadn't even laced the winter boots properly — she'd been in such a hurry to get out of the room, before she hurt someone, before she said something that would undoubtedly change all their futures forever, before she hurt herself.

Could that have anything to do with the fact that your feelings are pretty freaking strong?

Yeah, that was something to consider. Not only were her feelings strong, but now that she'd gone ahead and actually been with Lucas, with Lucas and Quinn at the same time, they weren't only strong, but also impossible to ignore.

Finally, she looked up. Maddy and Lily were both watching her, twin expressions of empathy and concern on their pretty faces. Because, of course, they'd both been where she was now, wondering *what the fuck?*, wondering *why the hell?* And it had worked for both of them, which was just about the only reason Ev was considering it, whatever the fuck *it* actually was, because she sure as shit didn't have a clue.

"I'm scared," she admitted. She'd chased serial killers down alleyways, rescued hostages in basements and gone head to head with some of the worst scum the world had to offer, and it was this, this baring of her heart and soul, this showing of vulnerability, this chance to get her heart thoroughly and completely broken, that scared her more than all the rest.

"Of what?" Lily's voice was kind and a little too knowing for Ev's taste. But Ev had seen the way Micah and Dec both looked at her — and more, for that matter, and there was no question in her mind that their relationship, and the one Maddy shared with Ryder and Christian, was as real as any she'd ever seen.

"All of it?" Ev shrugged. "Hell, I've only acknowledged to myself in the last five minutes that my feelings for Lucas are real, that the dreams I've been having are because I want him more than I'll allow myself to admit. This is new. It's a lot. And I'm really worried someone is going to get hurt." Because Ev knew to the depths of her heart that being the cause of a rift between the three of them, that hurting Quinn or Lucas or both of them, as was so very possible, would burn her worse than any pain she might endure herself. Heartbreak was almost inevitable here.

"When I first thought I had feelings for the guys," Lily said, "Maddy gave me some advice. The way we love, the way we live our lives — it's complicated, but it's not impossible. The trick is not having any secrets, no unanswered questions, any sense of not knowing the score. That's when you have trouble. If you want to know what the next step to take here is, Ev, that's a simple one. Go talk to them. See what they want. See how they feel. Work through it together."

She paused. "Or don't. You love Quinn and it's clear he loves you. If that's the life you want to lead, then follow that path. But if doing so makes it feel like you're ripping part of yourself in half, then there's your answer."

Ripping part of yourself in half. Yup, Lily knew *exactly* what was going through Ev's mind. Ev nodded.

"You're right," she said. Her voice cracked and Maddy smiled at her. Lily reached out and patted the top of her hand. "You're used to keeping all your emotions compartmentalized and organized and locked up tight, you think we don't get that? But this, this is going to take some unlocking to get through — and it'll be worth it, Ev. Because heads or tails, at least you'll know the score and you can move forward from there."

As Ev walked down the path and back toward her small guest house after hugging both Hollis women, who had departed in a rush to fix some wedding-related emergency, she thought about those last words Lily had shared. *At least you'll know.* That was surprisingly important, it turned out. Because she'd been living in an odd limbo, ever since she and Quinn had kissed for the very first time, not truly understanding how to share or organize her affections for the two most important men outside her family. Hell, to Ev they had always been family. And now she understood why. One way or the other, she'd finally know how to move forward.

She was so deep in thought she almost walked straight into someone who was coming up the path. Ev stumbled, tripped on a root covered in the new snow and landed square on her ass in a pile of the stuff. *Thank God there's still time for a shower before the wedding starts.*

Nursing wounded pride and a bruised butt, but nothing else, Ev went to right herself and apologize to whomever she'd walked into, when a hand appeared in front of her face. It was bare, no glove or mittens, despite the blistering cold, and the skin was rough and ragged, slightly discolored and a little bruised. It could have been a working man's hand, but before Ev could figure out what kind of working man, she looked up and saw Sam's brother, Zach Hawkins.

She nodded and took his hand, releasing it the moment she was steady on her feet. The man had a disconcerting gaze. It wasn't all that different from Sam's piercing blue eyes, but Sam smiled often and easily and made the color joyful and bright. On the man before her, the color was a stark, cold burn, seeping and hollow, like the frost all around them.

"I came down to your cottage to tell you that Quinn and Lucas are in Aimee's room," he said, and Ev realized she hadn't heard his voice once in the three days since their arrival. It was slow and gravelly and filled her with an odd sense of relief that they had crossed paths here on the walkway between the main houses and not when she was alone in her cabin. Not that she wasn't capable of defending herself, but there was no move to protect against the heebie-jeebies.

Scared of the boogey man too?

Lucas called it her Spidey-sense, but Ev just thought of it as good instinct, and something about Zacharias Hawkins had her hackles up. Well, *more* up, given that they'd been up since day one where the man was concerned. Still, she couldn't pin a guy for being a creep. Maybe she'd started looking for the worst in everyone. A job like hers could really do that to a person.

"Thanks for relaying the message," she said, a lot more cheerfully than she spoke on even the best day. He didn't move and she just gave him a big smile. "Anyway, it's an exciting day and I know we all have a lot to do."

After a moment of awkward silence, and maybe on purpose stretching it to the point where it wasn't just awkward but uncomfortable, Zacharias continued.

"Samantha wants you to come to her room when you're ready," he added. Then, finally, he turned around and started heading back up the hill. *Samantha*, that was odd. She'd been Sam for as long as Ev had known her, and the long-term instructors had all called her Sam, which meant the nickname couldn't have been new. She shrugged. Probably a leftover from their childhood. She still called Aurora a *two-faced, B-cup witch* when they fought.

Still, even as she headed down the rest of the path and began to prepare herself for the wedding, Ev couldn't help but think she was missing something where Zacharias Hawkins was concerned.

Chapter Thirteen

I'm scared.

Those words played over and over again in Quinn's mind, as he walked too quickly to Holmwood Manor and Aimee's room. Lucas was already there, undoubtedly flirting with Aimee's hot sisters. The call from Brandenwell had taken longer than Quinn had expected or wanted, to be honest, and he'd raced back to the cabin to find it empty, with a note from Lucas explaining that he'd gone to Aimee's room to prep the wedding party stuff and to come meet them as soon as he could.

That was it, nothing about the bomb of a confession Lucas had dropped on him not two hours earlier. Nothing about the secret his best friend had clearly been harboring for months, if not longer. Nothing about this cracked-ass plan to move across the country, back home, as far away from Quinn and Ev as he could get in the continental United States, and Lucas had never been one for the cold weather.

None of that. Just *Aimee wants the wedding party to meet early. Meet us when you can.* Scrawled below was Aimee's room number in Holmwood Manor.

And that was all before Quinn had overheard the conversation that brought his *today's been sort of complicated* level to DEFCON 1.

He hadn't been eavesdropping. The truth of the matter was that he had been fucking desperate to think about something other than the expression on Ev's face that morning, or the wretched look in Lucas' eyes. *I'm in love with her, man.* Because, *oh yeah*, Quinn fucking got how being in love with Ev Monteiro was just about enough to ruin a man. He understood that and then some.

And if the puzzle pieces fit, if he'd lined up all his numbers in pretty little rows and columns, then the only reason Ev shared a bed with him every night — well, every night they were home at the same time — was because of timing and some damn good luck. Nothing else. Because Quinn had started to suspect her reasoning for running off, for losing her damn mind over a night that should have been nothing more than fun entertainment, looked a lot like the reason Lucas wanted to move halfway across the world.

And that particular theory had been verified in neon lights when the conversation Quinn had *not been eavesdropping on* in order to clear his damn mind and put on a happy face for two of his best friends' wedding, had turned out to be the one where Ev seriously considered her feelings for them. Both of them.

I'm scared.

Because, of course, if she was somehow in love with both of them, Ev's only concern would be finding a way through the muck and madness to ensure none of them got hurt. Hell, he had no doubt in his mind that her wretched look, the desperation and the sadness and the fear, had a hell of a lot to do with his feelings.

Quinn tested himself. He thought about the way she had looked tucked into Lucas' warm embrace when he'd come back in from speaking with Lydia Brandenwell. Thought about what they had clearly done before falling asleep.

Lucas and Ev. Ev and Lucas. Together.

It made him feel...

Nothing.

Because until the night he'd kissed her, it had been Lucas and Ev and Quinn. It had been Ev and Quinn and Lucas. It had been Quinn and Lucas and Ev. The idea of bringing more emotion, deeper, more intense, erotic emotion into the mix, didn't feel nearly as uncomfortable as Quinn had expected it to.

Which, of course, made him feel more than a little uncomfortable. Men were supposed to stomp their feet and fight for their mates. For all intents and purposes, he should have been beating his chest, throwing Ev over his shoulder and telling Lucas to *hit the road, scram, LA isn't far enough.*

But not only did he loathe the idea of taking Ev's power from her — as if he'd ever even get the opportunity — but Quinn didn't want to do a damn one of those things.

I bet Ev could have a field day psychoanalyzing this.

This being the fact that the idea of his girlfriend and their best friend in bed together didn't scare him.

Fuck.

Because if it didn't scare him, at least, not nearly as much as he wanted it to, and Ev had already come to a dangerous conclusion of her own, then Lucas was the only holdout.

Jesus motherfucking Christ. How? How has it all gotten so fucking complicated in a matter of less than twelve hours?

But, of course, when he took the steps to the second floor of Holmwood Manor two at a time and thought over the last five years, Quinn knew this hadn't come about in twelve hours. This had come about the same way his own feelings for Ev had come about, over the span of months and years, over late-night pizza and watching reruns of *Saturday Night Live*, over the PTSD they all suffered for different reasons, but had weathered together, over the bond of the madness of their jobs, the rough life of an FBI agent, the empty apartment they all shared, the camaraderie of demanding families.

They had been friends first, but somewhere, for each of them, that had changed—so naturally and simply it had almost been imperceptible. Until Quinn and Ev had first kissed at the embassy party. Until they'd all made love together and he hadn't lost his damn mind from jealousy.

Which meant... Which meant it was time to face the music. Because if Lucas left, then he'd be taking part of Ev with him. Quinn had always been a confident man. He had the president's personal number in his cell. He won more cases than he lost. He was the second in command to Lydia fucking Brandenwell. He knew his own worth and exactly how hard it had been won.

But he also knew that whether or not Ev and Lucas knew it, if Lucas left for LA, if Lucas left *Ev*, then Quinn wouldn't be enough for her. In a way, the maddest, craziest, most insane sacrifice he'd ever considered making—and he'd walked empty-handed into more than a few terrorist situations — was also the most selfish. He couldn't lose Ev. And, in many ways, some related and some not, he couldn't lose Lucas either.

Which, of course, meant accepting something he'd never even considered before coming out here. Because if he couldn't accept it himself, then he sure as shit wouldn't be able to get Lucas or Ev to accept it either. After this wedding was over, tonight, when they were all happy and relieved and had time to talk, he'd bring it up. And if the thought that it might not work made his heart race and his palms sweat just a little, well, Quinn wasn't going to think too much about it. For now, though, he pushed all the madness from his mind. It was Sam and Aimee's wedding and they damn well deserved the happiest day ever, not a distracted groomsman. So he plastered an easy smile on his face, raised his hand and knocked on Aimee's door.

The mess hall cleaned up nicely. After comforting Ev in the barn, Maddy and Lily had turned their meeting and eating space into a winter wonderland, accentuated by the beautiful, sparkling snow outside. A silvery blue arbor had been set up before the fireplace, with droplets of glittering glass hanging from the top. Beside the awning was room for the wedding party, Aimee's to the right and Sam's to the left. The distinctions were arbitrary, since they'd all been a tight-knit group of friends from the start, but Ev's jaw had almost hit the floor when she'd first seen Lucas and Quinn standing beside Aimee's beautiful sisters, practicing their positions.

The soft silver color made Quinn's green eyes sparkle, bright and mischievous, and made Lucas look like a pirate with his long, dark hair. She had to admit that the shimmery silver dress she wore to stand on Sam's side of the ceremony made her feel a little like a princess. Or a warrior princess, since all the dresses had been accentuated with faux fur shawls and seriously kickass heeled winter boots. Ev could definitely get used to this style.

Of course, it was going to take a lot more than warrior princess boots to make her feel ready to have the conversation she'd told the Hollis sisters she was going to have. She wasn't scared by nature. Experiencing what she had at a young age, pushing herself hard to get the necessary degrees, going through strenuous training to get qualified and, of course, the horrors she witnessed pretty much on the regular, had all immunized her to the kind of fear most civilians felt. But this coming conversation, after the wedding had come to a close and she finally got the men to herself — it scared the ever-loving shit out of her. Because throughout all the rest, the memories of her childhood, the daily riot of hunting down serial killers, Lucas and Quinn had always been at her back.

Imagining trying to get through the rest of the nonsense without them was one of the scariest things she had ever faced. And more proof yet of how her feelings for both men were more complicated and deeper-reaching than friendship.

The room began to fill with people, friends, colleagues and family members, and Ev relaxed. Working in their field wasn't a solo deal. She always had people to lean on. She'd gotten through a lot because of the way that the system supported people. She'd be able to get through this.

Maybe you won't have to get through.

Her heart beat a little bit faster at the idea of maybe, just maybe, arguing her point before the two men and getting them to see it. At first, she'd been certain Quinn would be the holdout, but the more she had thought about it, the more she had realized that it would be Lucas who was difficult to win over, to make see sense. Instead of listening, he would probably tuck tail and run, to keep from hurting either of them. A cycle of self-sacrifice and all that. Communication, that was what Lily had said, and Ev knew if there was any way in hell and damnation she could make him see how this might, maybe, snowball's-chance work, it meant being honest.

It meant saying *I love you*.

Ev hadn't ever thought she'd say *I love you* to one man, let alone two. From the moment she'd known the FBI was her calling, she'd gone head down, late-nights-with-a-textbook double major. Her sisters had been her best friends because she had been too focused on her career and her future to spend much time out. Her happily-ever-after had been working for the BAU, not going off on the back of a horse into the sunset.

Well, it looked like things had changed.

The room was quieting down and Ev forced her attention away from the question of that inevitably difficult conversation to the wedding. Things hadn't always been easy for Sam and Aimee and they deserved the happiness of their friends and family surrounding them as they celebrated their love and future.

Aimee's side walked out first. Aimee's sisters, Quinn, Lucas, a slow progression down the aisle of decorated chairs and beautiful winter decor, until they were standing in a line beside the trellis. Then it was her turn, and she followed the two other women Sam had asked to be her bridesmaids, Macy and Carla, down the aisle, settling in her spot across from Lucas and Quinn.

Aimee walked down first, her arm looped through her father's. She wore a simple long-sleeved wedding gown with a lace bodice of sparkling beads and a blue throw over her shoulders, a delicate contrast to her dark skin. In short, she was radiant, but that had much more to do with the wide smile upon her face than the wrappings. She greeted each of them and the Justice, then stood below the trellis, waiting for Sam.

Ev wasn't used to the sight of Sam Hawkins in anything other than fatigues and T-shirts. She dressed casually, even when she wasn't working, and usually pulled her hair into a messy bun, when it grew long enough. But Sam had opted for a simple floor-length gown that made her appear young and ephemeral. She wore only light lipstick, her hair loose around her shoulders and her eyes just a touch watery.

Ev's eyes were starting to feel a little watery, too, because there was no doubt in her mind that Aimee and Sam were in love, deeply and truly, and they were all supremely honored to share their day of union.

Goodness, the romance of Wolf Creek, Montana, had definitely gone to Ev's head, because she'd never had a thought like that before in her life.

Until Quinn. Until Lucas. She glanced over at them, each so incredibly handsome, incredibly tempting in those beautiful suits, and they both seemed to feel her gaze, because they turned their heads to glance her way. The sensation of being looked at by both Quinn and Lucas, not just looked at, but *looked at*, admired, wanted, was overwhelming, and Ev's brain went into overload, dizzying and wanting and confused and...

Then the expression in both of their eyes changed and Ev's body went from hot to cold in an instant, because that wasn't the kind of expression any sort of FBI agent ever wanted to see on a fellow agent's face. Everything slowed, the room going into some sort of frozen, achingly glacial pace, even when Ev tried to swing her head around to see what was happening.

It glinted, in the light from the fire, in the soft glow from the snow outside, a .44 Magnum that, while relatively small for the guns she normally ran across, was most certainly capable of wreaking destructive havoc.

Gun. Origin. Perp.

Her brain sped up and the world around her melted away until she caught sight of the hand holding the gun, then the arm, then the man.

No wonder she'd recognized Zacharias Hawkins' expression. Seeing it now, rage, unmitigated, inexplicable, etched across otherwise soft blue eyes, wide cheeks curling into a furious growl, she knew that expression far, far too well. It had been on the faces of serial killers Penn Kingler, Darrell Sonnaise and Elliot Manaham. It had been on the faces of dozens of men and women she had helped to bring to justice over the last five years—ripe with anger, rich with injustice.

And it had been on the face of Peter Buldark the night she and Carly had held their breath in the closet and watched him kill Carly's parents and siblings. Buldark had turned, ax in hand, blood dripping between his fingers, and for a fraction of a heartbeat, Ev had thought he'd known they were in the closet. He'd practically stared right into her eyes, the same expression on his face that Zacharias wore now. Evil.

But whether he had known they were there or not, Buldark hadn't opened the closet door and come after them, and Ev refused to die now, refused to let a single other person she cared about, anyone in this room, die at the hands of a madman.

Lucas. Quinn. They were right in his path when he lifted his arm up, the gun clearly comfortable in his hand, as he stood calmly in the middle of the room, a stark contrast to the flower petals on the aisle beneath his booted feet, to the diamonds and snowfall all around them.

"Aimee, Aimee, Aimee." And he was toying with them, wasn't that wonderful? At least they now knew what the hell had been the cause of his aggression. Or rather, the focus of it. "You *dyke.*"

Confusion swamped Ev for a moment, and were it not for the adrenaline pumping through her veins and the insane man now wielding a gun at some of the people she cared about most in the world, then Ev would have actually laughed. Unkind words notwithstanding, Aimee's *dykeness* was in fact the reason they were at *her wedding* to *a woman.* Zacharias Hawkins' sister's wedding to be exact. Then, the confusion was gone as quickly as it had come.

Fucking bigot. This man standing before them all, in a room filled to the brim with FBI agents, detectives and the whole gamut of law enforcement, waiting for his next move with bated breath, was nothing more than a good old-fashioned bigot who, yup, there it was, blamed Sam's *sin* on Aimee.

"If you hadn't made my sister gay, my parents would still be alive."

Ev blinked at that particular statement and she was sure she wasn't the only one. Thankfully, good old Zacharias was there to explain.

"They were going to a *Pride parade*." He guffawed and the sound echoed in the large room, suddenly so cold and sparse, despite the beauty of the ceremony. "A surprise visit, right, Sammy?" At this, he turned to look at her, and Sam's eyes were daggers, harsher than Ev had ever seen them before.

"If you hurt a single person," Sam began, but it was clear Zacharias had a hold on her wrist she was afraid to break, for fear of what he might do when she angered him. Ev had no doubt in her mind Sam knew much, much more about her brother's anger than the rest of them did.

"Just one, *sis*," he began. "Just one person."

'One person', Ev's ass. Zacharias lifted the gun and the room came back into motion, too fast this time and in that moment not nearly fast enough. Because Ev saw the horror in Sam's eyes and she felt the knife deep in her heart at the idea of Sam losing Aimee on the day of her wedding. Then, in a panic of adrenaline and fear, that knife deep in her heart twisted and Ev's thoughts turned inwards to the horror down to the depths of her soul, if she were to lose Quinn.

If she were to lose Lucas.

Hawkins' face changed and she knew she was the only one with the right vantage point and knowledge to recognize it for what it was. In the same instant he brought the gun up, she took a running leap and thrust herself between him and the men she loved.

Sam took advantage of the distraction and wrestled the gun out from his hand in less time than it took Ev to get the wind back into her lungs. They burned with adrenaline with fear and panic and the rough scrape of oxygen. She pressed her hands against the floor to fight the swell of vertigo, but her heart pounded too quickly and the sounds of people around them came in and out of focus, like she was in some sort of tunnel, losing her signal.

But she wasn't a cell phone and it seemed like the sounds were getting further away, rather than closer. In fact, the more she tried to focus on what the people around her were saying, the more difficult it became.

"Jesus, Ev, you're bleeding." Sam's voice, she recognized. But there was no denying that it was laced with panic and she barked orders out, as she dragged her brother away, calling for...*a medic*. That couldn't be right. They weren't on any sort of battlefield. They were in...Colorado? Surely it wasn't Colorado. But there was snow outside. She could see it over the crowd of people around her. Sparkling, shiny, beautiful snow. She cocked her head to the side, but the view was obscured when someone stuck their face in front of her.

"Ev, look at me." Quinn's voice, now. "Ev, I swear to *fuck*." Just when he said that, she gave a little wobble and almost toppled from her knees to the hardwood floor, draped over with rose petals. That was odd. Why were there rose petals in Colorado in winter? Roses didn't grow in winter. Did they even grow in Colorado?

"Shh, I've got you, Evvie." That voice was familiar too. *Evvie.* Who called her that?

Lucas. Lucas that she was not in love with. Lucas that she *was* in love with. Oh God. *Oh God*, she'd never told him, never told either of them. And now she was probably going to die. The knowledge was there flat in the back of her mind, a series of facts and figures that added up to one obvious possibility. She was losing blood and fast, her head was woozy, her thoughts were most confused and Quinn looked worried. Of course, it was the worry on his face that hammered the point home, because Quinn didn't look worried. Not ever.

"Quinn." She tried to sit up, even though those same columns and facts and figures told her that sitting up was most definitely a bad idea. Still, she tried, and large hands pushed her gently back down, so she was pressed against Lucas' chest and breathing in the familiar scent of him. She loved this man, just as she loved Quinn, and she was going to die without ever having told him.

Like hell she was.

For a second, Ev actually believed it worked, that her anger had clotted the hole where the one shot Hawkins had gotten off had entered her...gut? It felt like it. But Ev knew well enough it wasn't the entrance that was the problem, but the whole big mess of organs down there that meant her body was trying desperately to die. She had no plan of going along without a fight.

"I'm here," Quinn told her, grabbing her hand. "We're both here. Don't you go anywhere, alright? We've got a helicopter on the way to take you to the ER, but you have to stay with us." Helicopter, another sign she was dying. Interesting.

"Quinn, I..." *What?* What was she saying? It had been on the tip of her tongue not a moment before but each passing breath was more painful, distracting from the fury and upset at dying here, like this, and she labored to get more air into her lungs.

"Shh, baby, I know. I love you, too. We both do."

That was important, but God, it was so hard to think, so hard to focus, and her vision was definitely blurring, like her hearing, going in and out until she couldn't focus on a single point anymore, not Quinn's face or the shiny snow outside the window.

Then it was her body moving, not only her mind, when Lucas carefully lifted her. His touch was gentle and soft, just as it had been when he'd made love to her that morning and Ev smiled, or tried to smile, though her body moved and jostled. Above her, she heard unfamiliar voices, then her body was lifted up from the ground and she was carried out of the room.

A stretcher. But she still wasn't going to die today. She'd determined that, lying between the two of them, and nothing had changed. She had to say it, had to tell them both the truth, they needed to know.

The medics loaded her onto the helicopter, the sound whomping in and out of her ears in slow motion, just the way Quinn and Lucas argued with the medics before climbing into the helicopter behind her, their faces both clenched so tight she wondered if they had been hurt. Of course, her body was going into shock, so nothing hurt her right now, not even a bullet wound.

She wondered if shock could dull a broken heart.

But it was hard to focus on why her heart might be breaking or if it was broken right now, especially when the medic placed something over her face and told her, in a distant, warping sound, to breathe and Ev took a few shallow breaths before everything, blissfully, went dark.

Chapter Fourteen

Quinn had actually punched the wall. Over the years of their friendship, Lucas had been well exposed to the tight leash Quinn Langston kept on his anger, to the control and the rigor he used to keep himself in check. Much of his internal riot had to do with the Middle East, stories Quinn very rarely told them about. This time, it had to do with Ev.

Ev, who had been rushed to St. Peter's Hospital in Helena after getting shot by a bigoted madman who'd brought a .44 Magnum as a wedding gift. Ev, who was in the operating room *right now* with a collapsed lung from the bullet wound she'd gotten saving Aimee's life. Saving their lives.

Lucas' heart hurt. Probably more than Quinn's hand, which was now on ice thanks to a terrified nurse who'd started *yes sir-ing* him when he'd flashed his FBI badge. Quinn had never abused that badge before in his life, but *normally* had gone out of the window when they'd stopped being certain Ev was going to live. Which was about .25 seconds after she'd leapt from the altar in a goddamned gown and tackled the bear of a man holding a gun.

Quinn stood suddenly, tossing the mostly melted ice pack onto a table in the waiting room and staring at the wall like it might give him answers the doctors couldn't. The heli ride had been short, but God, it had felt like a million years to rush her through the hospital doors and into the operating room. They'd been waiting in this sterile hell for over two hours and still they were no closer to Ev's recovery, to taking her home and... And what? Leaving.

Fuck if he knew now. He'd planned to leave, after all was said and done, but the thought of losing her made him sick, made it feel like it was *his* lungs collapsing and there was no surgeon or doctor who would be able to stitch him up.

He hadn't been exaggerating when he'd told Quinn that he loved this woman. In fact, he hadn't been nearly vehement enough, and now the truth, the potential that they might lose her — it burned him through.

"We need to talk, Lucas." Quinn spoke through clenched teeth, breathing like a bull and pacing. He approximated a smile at the receptionist, but, given the concerned look on her face, it was more of a grimace. "Is there a private room we could speak in? It's a matter of national security." *Wow, abusing my power twice in as many hours – I'm deteriorating quickly.*

She nodded and grabbed a circle of keys from a metal filing drawer, then led them down the hall to a dark room. When she unlocked it, the lights flickered on, and she didn't let the door hit her on the way out.

"You scared that woman half to death," Lucas said, leaning against the doorframe and watching his best friend. Quinn had resumed pacing. "And what's this 'matter of national security' bullshit? What couldn't we talk about out there, huh? What if they can't find us?" It wasn't good that both of their control was beginning to fray at the same time. Definitely, one hundred percent not good.

"Fuck…" Quinn rubbed his face and chin and when he moved his hands away, his green eyes sparkled with moisture. Lucas could relate. "There's something we need to talk about and it's private, okay? God, I was gonna wait to do this…" He shook his head. "Of course, I was gonna wait for *Ev…*"

He looked Lucas square in the eye then and everything else in that moment disappeared. No, Lucas hadn't jumped on the dick bandwagon, so to speak, but his love for Quinn Langston was there, brotherly love, intimate, special, deep and bonding love born from a lifetime of shared suffering—and shared joy. Lucas didn't know why, but something akin to relief washed over him. This was *Quinn*, for fuck's sake. With the exception of one pretty glaring example, they didn't keep secrets from each other.

"Are you asking her to marry you?" It was the first thing that had popped into Lucas' head and it made sense, in a doom and gloom sort of way. Of course, Quinn would want to give Lucas a heads-up before asking Ev to marry him, especially after all they hadn't talked about that morning…

But the expression on Quinn's face actually made an approximation of a laugh burst from Lucas' throat, despite the winding pressure around his neck telling him this was not going to be okay.

"No?" Quinn said it like a question. "I mean, of course one day I want to ask her. But that's… This is more complicated than that." He muttered something under his breath that sounded like a neat little package of all the words that couldn't be said on television.

"Jesus, Langston, whatever the fuck is going on, I can take it, okay?" Lucas almost said he'd had worse, but the truth was that the idea of losing Ev, even as just a friend, made his years on the force, his traumas and his darkness all feel a little less important.

"What I'm trying to tell you, it's crazy." Quinn rubbed his hands over his face. "Like fucking crazy. Like Ev would have a field day psychoanalyzing crazy."

Lucas didn't respond, only stared Quinn in the eye until he took a deep breath and continued.

"I think she wants us both," he said quietly. "Not *wants*, but wants to keep. I don't know, like the guys at the ranch and Micah and Dec, the trainers. I think she wants to *keep* us both." He scrubbed his face again. "And I've run over in my head a thousand times why that can't work, why I don't want that, why it's not *okay*." He winced at the word but barreled on. "And I can't come up with a goddamn thing, Lucas. You've loved her as long as I have. It was only a matter of timing that I said it first. And Evs, she loves you, too."

He leaned back against the far wall, smacking his head hard. "It's always been all three of us. You know it as well as I do. Crossing the line last night — all it did was make me realize that we need each other more than I thought. So I guess what I'm asking is…stay?"

Yeah, in all of that fucking bomb, Quinn was asking him to stay. Just to stay.

"You're asking more than that," Lucas said quietly, trying to wade through his thoughts, but goddamn, there were so many fucking thoughts and…

"Yeah." Quinn stood and started pacing again. "I'm asking you to stay and love Ev with me. I'm asking you to help me make her the happiest woman on this fucking planet day in and day out. I'm telling you, right now, if you walk out on DC, on her, on *us*, then she'll never be whole, man. And yeah, does it twist me up a little that I'm not enough for her? You know what, not as much as I thought it was going to."

It was possible this was the most talking Quinn had done all at once in the whole time Lucas had known him. Talking that he now had to fight through because what Quinn was asking, telling, it was crazy, it really was crazy. But not impossible.

A ferocious, uninhibited glimmer of hope burgeoned in his chest and Lucas took a deep breath to steady himself. He was a fucking federal agent, after all. He needed to think through this situation with logic and rationality.

"Why do you think she loves me, too?" he asked quietly. "Why do you think she'd want anything to do with something as crazy as this?" Because Quinn hadn't been wrong, this *was* crazy. And maybe even crazy enough to work too.

"Well, for one, I heard her talking to Maddy and Lily," Quinn explained. "I didn't mean to, I was actually trying to distract myself from the conversation with you, to be honest. But even if I hadn't heard her say a damn thing, I think I'd know. In fact, I'm pretty damn sure I've known for a while. It's what drove her out this morning and what's been on her mind for months now. Us all sleeping together, I think it pushed her over the edge."

It had damn well pushed Lucas over the edge.

But God, what the hell am I supposed to say to a proposition like this?

Yes, dammit. You say yes.

"How?" That was a much simpler question.

Quinn shrugged, apparently pleased they'd gotten this far.

"However she wants. I mean really, what changes? We already have the apartment and with the amount we're all home at the same time, it'll be enough to count as one relationship." The sound he made next was both self-effacing and relieved. "Listen, I know how insane this sounds, I really do. But it works for the Hollis sisters, both of them. And I can't help but think it's just one step further from what we've already got."

When Quinn puts it like that…

Lucas opened his mouth without a clue as to what he was going to say. Deep in his gut, he knew what he wanted. He knew he wanted to come home to Ev every night, to a home filled with love and joy, to take that one extra step and just love her together. After all, he totally got what it felt like to love Ev Monteiro.

But before he got the chance, before he could get a goddamned word out, his phone buzzed, angry, in his back pocket.

Sam.

His fingers actually shook as he accepted the call.

"She's out," Sam said without any preamble. "She's out, you can see her."

Time slowed in the moments it took for them to get up to Ev's room and Lucas lost track of everything but the need to see her, the need to touch her, to prove to himself she really was okay, that she would live.

Then what? He couldn't answer that question, couldn't possibly know what to think or say past seeing her face. Because what Quinn had asked of him, it wasn't a decision to be taken lightly. And though he'd said it was only the next step in their relationship, Lucas knew it could change everything. Hell, it had already changed so much.

But then the nurse was slowly letting them into Ev's room then leaving them to it, and everything triple-timed, making his heart feel full and tears spring to his eyes. She looked a sight, hooked up to tubes and wires. Her hair was messy and slick with sweat and she looked as if she'd gone three rounds with Godzilla, but God, she was beautiful.

Without making a sound, they took chairs on each side of her bed, and Ev slowly cracked her eyes open when Quinn placed his hand on hers. Her smile was weak, but so genuine it made Lucas' heart hurt.

"Hey there, superwoman," Quinn said, keeping his voice quiet and low. "How are you feeling?"

Her voice was a little dry and husky when she spoke, but she replied anyway, "Like I just got shot."

Lucas couldn't help it, he laughed, drawing her attention to him, those powerful brown eyes making him feel more than he'd allowed himself to feel in so, so long. Her expression changed almost imperceptibly, but Lucas knew her well enough at this point to see even the smallest details.

"Lucas." She reached her hand out to settle it on his, and her smile wavered. "There's something I need to tell you, both of you." God, she sounded so weak, and his blood ran hot with the need to protect her, no matter how capable she was of protecting herself.

"I love you, too." The words were out of his mouth before Lucas had time to process them with his brain. Ev's eyes went wide, but Lucas didn't stop, couldn't stop now. "God, Ev, I've loved you since the day you first kicked my ass in training, since you told us about Peter Buldark, since you insisted we all move in together and that we keep the place clean." He shook his head. "See, Quinn, he's got this crazy idea that we might just all be good for each other and, goddammit, I think he's right."

She turned to look at Quinn now, the motion costing her. "You knew?"

Quinn shrugged. "It took me a while, but I figured it out."

"And you're...okay with this? I mean, I don't know if *I'm* okay with this."

Quinn placed a gentle kiss on her forehead. "Ev, we love you. It's as simple and as complicated as that. I don't have any claim to you simply because I kissed you first. If Lucas leaves, if it's just you and me, we'll be happy, but not all the way happy. And God, I want you to be all the way happy."

Now her gaze was back on him. "You were going to leave." His face actually flushed, but he steeled himself.

"Before I knew, yeah. It was too hard for me to watch you guys together. I was going to take a job in LA but I don't think I'm going to do it now..."

And goddammit, if that didn't feel incredible to say, that he was staying here, with them, the two people he loved most in the world. Because yeah, he did love Quinn, trusted him to love Ev the way Lucas loved Ev, the way he always had. And Ev, God, his heart and soul had never felt so full, so incredible as right at this moment.

"Damn right, you're not," she said. "I don't care about the hows and whys and wherefores. All I need to know is that when I come home at night, it's to both of you. God, you've made the nightmares go away, together. With you by my side, Quinn, Lucas, I feel like I can take on the whole world."

"You don't need us for that," Quinn said. "But we'll damn well be by your side."

They were both holding her hand, perhaps a little too tightly, when Ev fell asleep. And they stayed like that, in the hospital room, for a damn long time. Because it had been too long of not knowing, of pretending their feelings were different than they were. They had wasted more than enough time already. And now, with he and Quinn a united force to love Ev for as long as she would let them and longer, and with Ev herself promising a life of shared happiness, of togetherness and completion Lucas had only ever dreamed of, Lucas knew deep in his heart that, though unusual, their relationship was perfect. Because when she woke, this time in the hospital and for all the times to follow, each morning and each late-night call into work, she'd be waking to love both of them, the two men who would always be by her side. Together forever.

And if Lucas felt a little bit of moisture slide down his cheeks at the thought of it, he didn't bother to wipe it away, not even when Quinn saw him. Because Ev was alive, and despite the horror and bullshit they'd all endured in their lives, they were finally getting their shot at happiness. And it came with a whole lot of extra love.

Epilogue

"All right, I think I understand the appeal of Montana now." Ev stood at the top of the hill, overlooking a yawning valley with great swaths of green ribbons cutting through the view. The air was sweet with wet earth and early growth and, though it was far from warm, she was comfortable in her light jacket and content to stare out at the view for a good long time.

"I don't know, I like the view from where I'm standing." Quinn shook his head when Lucas shot her an overly flirtatious wink. Or rather, it would have been an overly flirtatious wink a year ago. Now it just made her body heat against the spring breeze and a familiar ache blossom in her chest. Would she ever stop wanting these men? Would she ever stop feeling grateful to the universe for sharing them with her, giving them all a chance at happiness?

Nope. To both questions.

"Mine isn't so bad, either," she responded, her out-of-character giggly mood inspired by the fresh air, the upcoming nuptials and the chance to see Lily and Maddy Hollis again. And, of course, the low current of incredible joy that ran through her day in and day out knowing Quinn and Lucas would both be waiting for her when she got home at the end of it.

From the moment in the hospital room when they had all agreed to give their crazy love a chance, Ev's life had become the kind of bright and beautiful place she'd only ever read about. Sure, their jobs were all difficult to bear more days than not, but the knowledge that they weren't doing it alone, that they were never fighting their ghosts alone again, had made all the difference. She had moved back into her old bedroom, the one they'd converted into an office after she and Quinn had first started dating, and the arrangement worked nicely. They all had their space, room to be apart when the time called for it, but they shared the big bed in her room every night, and Ev knew she would never feel safer than during the time she spent pressed between her lovers.

"Don't look at me with that expression, Monteiro," Lucas chastised. "It gets me all hot and bothered."

Of course, dating Lucas hadn't exactly made him any less flirtatious. In fact, she could argue it had even made him worse. The difference was that now he focused all his attentions on her. He came to stand by her and Quinn walked to her other side, slowly wrapping an arm around her waist in his silent appreciation for her. That was another reason why they had all worked so well, why their friendship and their romance were so symbiotic and important. Completion and support—they all gave each other what they needed.

And right now, she needed *them*. Because just standing in their proximity, back in the very first place where Quinn and Lucas had claimed her through the night, back to the very first place where she'd ever made love with Lucas—which, of course, was what it had been—sent desire bursting through her body and made Ev incredibly aware of how close she was standing to her two very gorgeous partners, who would be more than willing to come at the sight of her crooked finger. Then come a few more times over the course of the weekend.

But before she got the chance to test her theory, Ev's name cut through the fresh morning air, and she turned away from Lucas and Quinn to see the Hollis sisters and their gaggle of gorgeous men climbing the small hill to greet them.

"I can't believe it!" Lily caught up to her first. "I mean, last time you were here, my God, you look fantastic."

Ev gave her a huge hug. "I'm hoping tomorrow's ceremony is a lot less eventful than the last try," she said. "And I feel good! Doc says full recovery and no lasting damage. I had to do some PT for a while, but I'm back to my old self again."

Lily's grin was radiant. "Of course, it doesn't hurt to have two hot nursemaids taking care of you, does it?"

Ev snorted at the same moment Dec McCormick shot Lily a dark, promising glance. "I heard that, Lils…"

"Can you picture either Quinn or Lucas in scrubs? No thanks." She glanced over at her men—her men!—and laughed again. "There's so much freaking testosterone on this hill I'm surprised it's still standing."

Maddy joined them. "Now I'm imagining them *all* in nursemaid uniforms. I could see that working for Dec," she said, cocking her head to the side when they both snorted even harder.

Over the months since Ev had been shot and they'd agreed to take their relationship to a new place, she'd been in fairly good touch with Maddy and Lily Hollis. It wasn't just only they were expert tour guides at navigating the trickier elements of this new dynamic, but she'd grown to care quite a lot for both of them as they'd exchanged messages and social media chats. Their friendship had also forced Ev to acknowledge that she didn't have much of a social life beyond work and Quinn and Lucas, and she was secretly pretty proud of how well they'd kept in touch.

"I have news!" Maddy whispered, her voice suddenly low and conspiratorial. "But you can't freak out. Promise."

Ev narrowed her eyes. "Do I look like the type of person to freak out?" she asked.

"Remember we found you crying in the barn not too long ago," Lily pointed out. "No secrets from us! But I'm shutting up now," she finished when Maddy sent her the evil big-sister eye.

Instead of saying anything, though, Maddy simply reached out and took Ev's wrist, before slowly guiding her hand to her stomach.

It was still fairly flat, but there was no denying the small curve low in her belly and the glow of Maddy's smile.

"Holy shit," Ev managed to breathe. "Holy shit!" She gathered Maddy into her arms in a careful but excited embrace, dancing them around in a circle, before holding Maddy back and looking at her, first her very smiling face, then down to her still-flat belly where they would be bringing a new generation of joy and love into the world.

"You said you wouldn't freak out!" Maddy said, but she was smiling too, even when their commotion brought the men over to investigate.

Ryder Dean slid his arm possessively around Maddy's waist then the lot of them laughed when Christian Harlow one-upped him and kissed her passionately and intensely on the lips.

"You told her, then?" Christian murmured against her mouth. "That we're having a baby?" He turned to catch Ev's eye. "She wanted to tell you in person. Now I understand why." Quinn and Lucas both clapped the men on the back and offered Maddy hugs and wide smiles, and it struck Ev for a moment that, though she'd probably never have a family like this—she'd never have babies in the traditional way, not with her age and the expectations of not just her job, but Lucas' and Quinn's jobs as well—she had, in many ways, gained a whole new family by coming out to the Triple Diamond Ranch.

"So is it going to come out wearing a Harley jacket or a Ford T-shirt?" Lucas quipped. "Ooh, in-family rivalry!"

Christian shook his head. "I don't care who the baby looks like, as long as it looks like Mads."

Ryder echoed the sentiment and pulled Maddy against him, and Ev's eyes felt surprisingly moist.

"We should probably let you get the rest of the wedding preparations covered," she said after a moment. "And I need a shower after the flight."

It was crazy, how she still felt the heat of their gaze when she mentioned something like *shower*, but feel it she did.

"Of course!" Maddy went from friend to business owner in a heartbeat. She fished the key out of her front pocket and tossed it to Ev. "You know where to find us this weekend. We still haven't dished about the hot nursemaids."

Ev gave them each another hug, even as Lucas muttered under his breath about *not being a piece of meat*, then she and her men were headed down the familiar path to the cabin they'd first shared months ago in this beautiful escape. She unlocked the door and walked over to the fireplace to get the place warmed up against the spring chill. Not that she needed warming, since there were two scandalously hot federal agents willing to do exactly that the moment she asked them for it.

"Now this is a sight I could get used to." It was Quinn who spoke, just as it had been Quinn that first night. Quinn, who had the most to lose, who had guided them all through the rough waters.

"You're not bored yet?" Ev asked, getting down on her knees before the fireplace and, yeah, maybe sticking her ass a little too far up in the air.

Lucas touched her first. She'd been able to tell their touch within a matter of nights together. Quinn's control was veiled and somehow desperate at the same time. Lucas kissed with abandon, without pause or control. They varied, but she knew. She always knew.

"Some days, I wish I could watch you grow larger with our child," Lucas murmured low in her ear. Ev went to protest, but he beat her to it. "I know, I know. But God, Evvie, you reduce me to a caveman. Me Tarzan, you Jane."

She stood and wrapped her arms around his neck. "Okay, wild man, what do you have in store for me today?

He kissed her. She shouldn't have been surprised about that. Lucas' kisses were hot and demanding and, even after four months, Ev still wasn't able to get enough of them. Especially when Quinn came up to stand behind her, a solid, immovable mass of hard muscle, now leaning down to kiss her neck, her chest, the slope of her ear, whatever he thought would garner the most reaction from her. Which was, of course, exactly what he wanted.

"You looked at me that way," Lucas told her, temporarily distracting from Quinn's dangerous fingers and tongue and kisses.

Ev knew exactly what he was talking about, but she wanted him to say it. "What way?" she asked innocently.

"Like you're going over the *Kama Sutra* in your head and we're in the starring roles."

She shrugged. "Maybe I am. What should we try first?"

Quinn's movement hurried and he slipped his fingers up her shirt, across her back, spanning her ass with controlled, fluid, deadly motion. He knew what she needed and exactly how to give it to her, and it always made her anticipation mount higher, hotter and more and she burned for his touch, his kiss, his body deep inside hers.

"I think we should probably try fucking you in front of the gorgeous window this time," Quinn muttered, as if he were talking about something totally inane and not a surefire way to drive her completely fucking crazy with words alone.

"I'm all for a little public display of affection. In fact, turn around, Evvie." Lucas' voice was low and deep and a little dangerous, and he grinned at her with promise and power.

Ev did as she was told — she'd actually been listening to the people in her life a lot more ever since listening had started bringing orgasms with it. She turned and allowed Lucas to stroke her behind over the fabric he pulled taut, until he had fully explored the shape of her pussy with his hand and Ev was breathing hard, desire for this man, for these men, in every breath she took. She loved them both too much to ever hide the need they both inspired within her and she spread her legs to welcome more of their shared touch, as she always would.

"So beautiful." Quinn had breathed the words, but it was Lucas who was touching, stroking her, making her clench the back of the sofa like she had done all those months ago, only now it wasn't just for one night, now it wasn't a *just until morning* — now she had the two men who loved her most in the world and they were about to show her exactly how much that was.

So instead of rushing them, instead of demanding they give her the satisfaction she so desperately craved — always, always craved when she was around them — Ev let herself be pampered, touched, kissed and licked until starlights of pleasure popped before her eyes. She let herself be guided, half-carried by the two men, into the bedroom, where they flung the curtains open and gave in to their shared, depraved fantasy, filling her at both ends before the open window. Then she let them pull her back onto the couch and fill her again, together, Lucas below her and Quinn above, until she was tangling her hands in one of each of theirs and screaming a string of their names, wrapped in curse words, until her first release and her second washed over her whole body, barreling through her and her third third dragged both men with it and they all found that impossible pleasure, crashing hard over the edge together, shouting, whispering, moaning, breaking apart in each other's arms.

They finally all fell, sated, overwhelmed into a pile on the bed. Ev settled herself between the two men, her breathing still heavy, her body still wracked with the roiling aftermath of her pleasure, and she cuddled up against her two men, Quinn on one side, Lucas on the other, and she knew. No matter what life brought them — and in their line of work, life brought them a whole hell of a lot — no matter what dangers they faced or tragedies they witnessed, no matter the world they worked in every day, they could get through every single challenge, they could best each obstacle. Because when the three of them were together — and Ev planned for the three of them to be together for a damn long time — they could accomplish anything.

Want to see more from this author?
Here's a taster for you to enjoy!

Triple Diamond:
Heart of the Storm
Gemma Snow

Excerpt

And there goes the floor.

Sawyer always knew when the floor was about to collapse. In the din of the fire, the roar compounded by the fishbowl of his helmet and oxygen mask, he couldn't hear much beyond angry, sharp sounds of chaos, a wardrobe falling over, glass shattering. He never *heard* the floor beneath his feet begin to give, but he damn near almost always felt it, and it precipitated a real bad scene each and every time it had happened to him.

Time to move ass, Matthews.

Because they were missing one of the Hemwick children and he'd be damned if he let anything happen to the kid on his watch. But he'd already been inside the ranch house for two, maybe three minutes and they hadn't arrived on the scene for at least six or seven after the call had come in.

But Sawyer wasn't the type to play at odds. A wrong-side-of-the-tracks, school-paid-lunches kid like him knew that placing any sort of belief in a higher system was bound to end in disaster. So he stuck to the cold — hot — hard facts and to the very tangible things he could do with the resources right in front of him.

Like walking down the hall and away from the cracking floorboards. The door at the far end of the hallway was shut and Sawyer hoped like hell that the missing child was in that room, and not any of the three open doorways he'd passed on his too-slow walk. If they had been, he was too late. He got to the door after what felt like an eternity and jangled the knob.

What's behind door number four?

Hopefully, April Anne Hemwick.

Heat from the blaze around him had warped the wood and he came at it from the side, shoving the weight of his body against the door until it finally pushed free of the jamb. Thankfully, it didn't break, and when one glance around the room told him that the fire hadn't yet spread inside, he quickly pushed the door closed again. The air was smoky and thick, but there weren't any discernable flames and that gave him hope. If April Anne had been in this room when the fire started, she might just be okay.

Just as with the crunch of the floorboard beneath his feet, it was intuition, instinct and experience, rather than a discernable sound, that pulled him to the far corner of the room. He crouched low and through the haze caught sight of a flash of pink and blue. He tapped her on the leg and she turned, *thank fuck*, and he realized she was holding something. Two somethings.

Kittens. Fucking wonderful.

It was challenging enough bringing a four-year-old down from the second story of a burning house, but add kittens to the mix?

Doesn't matter.

It didn't matter. He lifted April Anne from the ground and pressed her face into his chest, the kittens squished between them, before walking three short steps to the window. Most of his team was down below and he pushed the window open easily enough, drawing attention to their position with a quick wave. One of the engines was brought quickly to the other side of the house and Jensen was practically halfway up the ladder by the time it hit the window. He took April Anne from Sawyer's arms and Sawyer scooped the two kittens from her hands so that she could properly hold on to Jensen on the descent. Then he, too, began climbing his way back down until he felt the hard, sold metal of the engine under his feet, then the ground below that.

By the time he got his helmet off, a challenge with the squirming kittens now both held by their scruffs in one hand, April Anne was in her mother's arms and the six Hemwicks had gathered together in a massive hug before turning to watch the second floor collapse and the house begin to implode right before their eyes.

"It's okay." Daniel Hemwick was holding his son's hand and stroking his wife's back. "We're all okay. The things are just things, but we still have each other."

It wasn't an unfamiliar sentiment to hear at a site like this one, but it still made something in Sawyer's belly clench in an uncomfortable way, and he tried not to focus on all the reasons that might be. Waiting until he would no longer interrupt the moment, he walked over to the family and knelt before April Anne, then extended the two kittens in his hand.

She pulled free of her mother's grip and caught him around the neck, hugging him so tightly that it nearly knocked Sawyer to his ass. This little girl had just gone through hell and she still packed a powerful punch — he only hoped he'd be so lucky one day.

"Thanks, Spider-Man," she said, then took the two kittens and hugged them close before handing them to her mother. He'd take Spiderman. It was one of the most recent superhero blockbuster films, and with long red hair and freckles to his hairline, he hardly passed for the King of Wakanda. He pulled his gear off his hand to ruffle her hair, then turned to her parents.

"I'm sorry about your house," Sawyer said. It was true — he may have been a brusque, cynical s.o.b., but it was hard to feel anything other than sympathy for a family who had just lost so much.

"Nothing to be sorry about," Daniel Hemwick said. He extended his hand and Sawyer was surprised to find the man's grip was strong, despite everything their family had experienced that night. "You saved our April Anne. That's the only thing that matters, Chief."

The Spiderman praise from a four-year-old, he could handle. This was edging on too gushy for him, but Sawyer held the man's gaze, nodded to Jenny Hemwick, whose eyes were glassy with unshed tears, then turned away from the family to head back to his engine. Jensen was sitting on the back bumper, chugging a bottle of water, and he handed one to Sawyer, who drank it down greedily.

Before they had the chance to exchange a word, however, Jensen's eyes sparked at something behind him and Sawyer's hackles rose.

"Chief." This was not said in the same tone that Daniel Hemwick had used. Sawyer bit the inside of his lip, not bothering to hide his grimace when he turned to face Cade Easton.

Lewis and Clark County Sheriff Cade Easton was the day to Sawyer's night, if day and night enjoyed squirting each other in the eye with lemon juice and rubbing it in with salt. Where Sawyer's hair was long and red, Cade wore his just shy of military style. Where Sawyer made a habit of running into burning buildings – quite literally playing with fire – Cade ensured that law and order were upheld, to a nauseating degree in their tiny, nearly crimeless county. Cade was a stickler for rules Sawyer had never had any trouble breaking, and the only time Sawyer had seen him behave as anything less than a proper fucking gentleman was when he was poking at Sawyer's bruises that would otherwise have healed a long time ago.

"Sheriff." This in a very specific tone from Sawyer, who had very little difficulty stooping to Easton's level where pettiness was concerned.

"Glad to see the kittens of Wolf Creek remained unscathed," Easton said drily. "I have to get your statement."

Instead of replying, Sawyer took a long drink from the water bottle Jensen had handed him, taking some perverse pleasure in making the sheriff wait. Cade didn't need his statement right now any more than they needed a match, but he liked making a show of being the big gun in town, as if Sawyer's team were the cleanup crew and he owned the mansion.

"You'll get my statement tomorrow, Easton," Sawyer said after an intentionally long pause. "Just come on down to the station to pick it up."

Easton didn't miss a beat. "Now, Chief," he said. "Don't make this harder than it needs to be." They were in each other's faces now — for *fuck's* sake, how did they always end up in each other's faces? — and Sawyer only realized he was clenching his jaw when it began to throb in time with the pounding of his heart.

When did it get like this?

When had it gotten like this? They had never been friends, not really, but the stark animosity between them was a hell of a lot stronger now than it had been back in the beginning. Sure, two fucked-up kids from the wrong side of town were either gonna scuffle or have each other's backs, and it was clear that best friends they would never be, but it shouldn't have been this fucking hard to have a goddamn conversation without it nearly coming to blows.

You know exactly when it got to be like this.

Yeah, and Sawyer was about as likely to admit it as he was to get down on one knee and propose to Cade Easton.

"Did someone forget to take his happy pills today?" Sawyer prodded, taking perverse pleasure in watching the fury behind Easton's eyes. Running the Wolf County Fire Department took some of the edge off the rebellious streak that had plagued him since childhood, but pissing people off — especially Easton — was a goddamn fun way to pass the time.

"I'm not the one who needs happy pills. But if you want someone to buy your Viagra, you can just ask," Easton replied. "I'm sure we can get you back to rights no problem."

"Maybe if you spent half as much time running chasing down criminals as you do thinking about my dick, you'd feel better about yourself."

"I'd say you're stooping low, but word about town is that you're packing short," Easton replied with a smug grin.

Sawyer grunted to cover the laugh. It helped when his regular sparring partner was actually capable of delivering serious blows, and though he'd never admit aloud, Cade Easton could be one funny fuck. But before Sawyer had the chance to think up some retort that would put an end to their inane bickering, he caught sight of a woman walking under the *caution* tape. His vision narrowed and Easton, Jensen and everything around them disappeared to background chatter. Nothing else mattered. Nothing else had ever mattered.

Hollie was back.

Home of Erotic Romance

Sign up for our newsletter and find out about all our romance book releases, eBook sales and promotions, sneak peeks and FREE romance books!

About the Author

Gemma Snow is the author of several works of erotic and romantic fiction in both the contemporary and historical genres, and enjoys pushing the limits of freedom, feminism, and fun in her stories. She has been an avid writer for many years, and recently moved back to her home state of New Jersey from Boston, after completing her education in journalism and creative writing.

In her free time, she loves to travel, and spent several months living in a 14th century castle in the Netherlands. When not exploring the world, she likes dreaming up stories, eating spicy food, driving fast cars, and talking to strangers.

Gemma loves to hear from readers. You can find her contact information, website details and author profile page at https://www.totallybound.com